THROUGH
THE FOREST

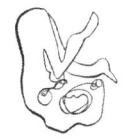

Laura Alcoba is a writer, translator and lecturer at the Université Paris-Nanterre. Author of numerous novels, she has also published translations of authors as diverse as Pedro Calderón de la Barca and Fernanda Melchor. She has won many prizes for her work and her books have been translated into languages from all over the world.

Martin Munro is Winthrop-King Professor of French and Francophone Studies at Florida State University, having previously worked in Scotland, Ireland, and Trinidad. In 2023, he published a translation of Michaël Ferrier's *François, a Portrait of an Absent Friend* with Fum d'Estampa Press.

This translation has been published in Great Britain
by Fum d'Estampa Press Limited 2024
001

© Editions GALLIMARD, Paris, 2022
All rights reserved.

English language translation © Martin Munro, 2024

The moral rights of the author and translator have been asserted
Set in Minion Pro

Printed and bound by Great Britain by CMP UK Ltd.
A CIP catalogue record for this book is available from the British Library

ISBN: 978-1-913744-43-4

This book is sold subject to the condition that it shall not, by way of trade or otherwise, be lent, resold, hired out or otherwise circulated without the publisher's prior consent in any form of binding or cover other than that in which it is published and without a similar condition including this condition being imposed on the subsequent purchaser.

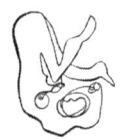

THROUGH
THE FOREST

LAURA ALCOBA

Translated from French by

MARTIN MUNRO

...something similar to those circles of Dante's purgatory immobilized in a single memory, and where are remade in a more constricted center the acts of past life.

> GÉRARD DE NERVAL,
> *Walks and Memories*
> "Chantilly"

CLAUDIO

Paris, December 1984

That day, Claudio did not listen to Griselda.

It was one of the first things he said to the lawyer. A year and a half later, when the trial took place, it was still one of the first things he said: that day, Griselda called him but he couldn't bear to listen to her.

He had, however, gone to find her before finishing his work, in that classroom he was going to paint, in one of the buildings of the school where they lived. Suddenly, he dropped everything. To discover all three of them, in the dark, at the back of the lodge.

*

He sees himself again, the same day, a few hours earlier, squatting in front of a large wall. He was putting on the last coat, hoping to finish before evening. When Griselda called to him from the doorway, Claudio was going over some green paint with his roller.

Standing in the doorway, Griselda said she didn't feel well. She had spoken in Spanish, the words she said were: "*No me siento bien, Claudio, vení…*"

Claudio barely turned around.

Flavia was at school; the boys were probably taking their nap. What did she want?

Still squatting, and already annoyed with her, he cast a furtive glance at her over his shoulder. Damn, that make-up… For several days, Griselda had been wearing far too much make-up.

Every morning, she put a mask on her face.

Claudio got up to reload his roller and took a few steps so he could admire the entire pistachio-green wall. Or maybe it was an even deeper green. The day before, the art teacher had passed by to see the worksite of the classroom she was soon to occupy. She had been surprised: "But that's so much deeper than pistachio, that's almost a chartreuse green, Claudio, where did you get that green from?" Then she'd laughed, amused. She would never have gone for such a deep green, but had to admit that it was not bad, not bad at all. For the skirtings, Claudio had chosen a deep plum, a color he had struggled to get hold of, but which, by way of experimenting and trying new mixes, had ended up being as intense as the one he had imagined when he first saw the gray room they had entrusted to him. When it came to colors, Claudio always knew what he wanted. At first the combinations he came up with seemed outlandish; but once they were on the walls they always worked, and everyone was happy.

That day in the doorway Griselda was motionless, lit by the pale light of the large window in front of her. Behind Griselda, the hallway was plunged into shadow which is probably why, despite the pale whiteness of the December light, you could see only her: like when an actor in a darkened theater hall emerges alone at the back of the stage.

In the doorway, she repeated her call: "*No me siento bien.*"

Claudio's eyes quickly glanced at her legs, her chest, but this second time he didn't look at Griselda's face. He didn't want to see her lips again, or her cheeks, or her eyelids. For they were as dark as the skirting board. It was one thing to let loose on a wall, okay, but on your own face, like Griselda did, he couldn't stand that.

Then, suddenly turning his back on her, he replied curtly, it's true. It's that he wanted her to go away, to return to the lodge, for the make-up-covered face in the doorway to disappear.

Claudio asked Griselda to leave.

But in truth, it was more than that.

He later said so to the lawyer, when they tried to reconstruct how the events had unfolded. In fact, Claudio sent her packing that day. As his eyes fell again on the mask that Griselda wore for a face, he felt a great anger rising in him. Abruptly turning his head away, he said something to her like: "Just beat it, will you!" Yes, what Claudio had said that day to Griselda, in Spanish, could be translated more or less as that. Like slamming a door in someone's face.

When did Griselda's broken voice come back in his memory? When did he first think again of her grim face right at the back of the stage, that mask calling out to him? Was it only after the fact, when he tried to reconstruct that day? Or on the day itself, when he was finally about to go see her, just across the yard?

He knows that suddenly, several hours after Griselda turned back, he left the worksite, hurrying to reach the lodge that served as their apartment. He crossed the empty yard. Most of the high school students had left, only two or three rooms upstairs were still lit. It was afternoon, but winter was approaching. So, even though it was afternoon, night was already closing in.

Claudio did not need to take his key out of his coat pocket. It was cold but the door was open.

In the lodge, the lights were off, everything inside was silent.

He remembers calling Griselda, then the children. Several times.

In the dark, Claudio saw his breath freeze to form two small white clouds.

Then, at the back of the darkened room, he caught sight of them.

*

Claudio had been living there for more than six years with Griselda and their three children.

A ground floor on to a large courtyard, where the high school students took their recess. The yard was then filled with laughter and shouts. Their lodge too, inevitably. When it was time for recess, they could barely hear each other speak in their own home. But the rest of the time, the place was extraordinarily quiet. Beyond the benches, at the far end of the courtyard, there was a small, enclosed garden that they had looked after since they'd worked as caretakers at T. High School. The little garden was surrounded by a railing: the students had no access to it. It looked like a miniature square, kept especially for them. Claudio had planted several rosebushes there. In a corner of the garden, against the railing, he had even laid out a vegetable patch. They may have only been the caretakers at T. High School, but this garden was their garden.

Yes, it does seem to him that at some point on that Friday he thought again of Griselda's face calling to him from the doorway. Otherwise, why would he suddenly have left everything behind?

Claudio was kneeling as he painted the skirting boards again. He had almost finished the last coat; it wouldn't take him much longer. But he suddenly got up, mechanically cleaned his brush, hastily took off his overalls and put his clothes back on. Then he left, when he was almost done, but not quite. Suddenly, he quickened his steps.

Despite the cold, the door to the lodge was open.

The light was off, everything inside was silent.

He remembers calling Griselda and saying the children's names.

It was only afterwards, at the back of the dark room, that he caught sight of them.

Griselda was on the floor between the sofa and the table, more or less on her knees, her head bowed. The boys were lying on their backs on the sofa. The cushions that were normally used to sit back on the wall side had been slid under their heads. The children were side by side, dressed in their white bathrobes. The toweling belts had been carefully tied around their waists, forming two perfectly regular and identical loops.

Then he noticed the water.

Despite the darkness, Claudio saw two large halos under the boys' hair. He put out a hand. The cushions that served as their pillows were damp and cold.

Claudio bent down; he took Griselda by the shoulders. She too was soaked. They looked like three shipwreck victims. Claudio shook Griselda. She seemed to be sleeping soundly. He shook even harder, but Griselda's head was bobbing all over the place, as if Claudio had nothing but a rag doll in his hands. He repeated her name. He must have screamed.

Griselda finally opened her eyes, but she looked at him without a word, as if she did not recognize him, through the powder and make-up that had run down her face. Then Claudio left the lodge. He does not know how he managed to take those steps. In the courtyard, he came across the man he always saw with files under his arm. But he did not understand what Claudio was telling him, he saw only his terror. The man entered the room. It was he who called the emergency services. Shortly after, the firemen arrived.

What he still remembers is the metallic sound of the helmets and the boots in the middle of the courtyard.

The firemen tried to revive Boris. It was too late for Sacha.

When the police arrived, it was pitch dark. It had been so for a long time already.

FLAVIA

November 2018, at Le Bûcheron

It was long ago, of course. Very long ago, even.

It was November 1, 2018, and the memories Flavia was recalling dated back to December 1984. At the time, she was only six years old.

"And I have just turned forty!"

She said those words with a smile, looking amused. Perplexed, too. As if her fortieth birthday a few weeks earlier continued to be a surprise to her. As if she herself doubted that the thing could have happened to her.

I was perfectly aware that she had recently turned forty. I had already been carrying out my investigation for several months. Maybe even longer than that, in fact, when I think about it. In any case, in my notebook, I had long since noted everyone's date of birth, including hers.

But when she told me about her birthday at Le Bûcheron, the café in the Saint-Paul district where we had arranged to meet, I too suddenly had a hard time believing it. Forty years! With her big black eyes, her smooth, luminous face, Flavia looked ten years younger. Even younger than that, to be honest. Her straight brown hair hung loosely. Everything about her suggested a natural youthfulness. Short and petite, in her straight jeans and flats, she looked like a teenager.

"Well, yes, but however you look at it, I'm still forty years old…"

She was only six at the time of the event we were talking about.

So, it was awfully long ago, for sure.

Many things seemed fuzzy to her or somewhat unreal, as happens with very old memories that, over time, take on the air of fiction.

But Flavia was sure about some things.

First, that it was a Friday.

Friday, December 14, 1984, to be exact.

If she knows the exact date, it's because she saw it later in her parents' family record book, next to her brothers' names. But it is her memory that tells her that December 14, 1984 was a Friday. No need to check it in an online calendar, she is sure about it.

She had been in preparatory class for a little over three months. Maybe a few weeks since she had learned to read, not much more. She remembers: one day, sight-reading had ceased to be hard work, suddenly in her schoolbook she had no longer seen letters, but words and even parts of sentences that she understood. Shortly before that Friday, the words had gone in through her eyes and she had been proud of herself.

"Do you have any other memories? Of this Friday, in particular?"

Yes, she did have some.

Flavia knew that I intended to write a book about these events, and she wanted to share with me what her memory had retained of them. For my book, and in fact for her too, she really wanted to talk to me about that day.

That's how Flavia refers to it: *that day.*

The thing is that she too had been thinking about it a lot for a few months, just when I turned up out of the blue to ask her questions... It was strange, like a coincidence, but this appointment with me came at the right time.

Flavia paused. Then she said to me, lowering her eyes, as if suddenly disillusioned:

"At the same time, for other people, it's just a news item…"

"Not for me. I don't see it as only a news story. I knew you; I would like to understand."

Flavia looked at me, then she gave a brief smile, as if she was smiling to herself.

She continued.

She still had a few images from that day. Some very precise images, as if they had been engraved in her memory.

As Flavia spoke, I took notes in the notebook that lay open between us on the coffee table.

Some of those memories were like the fragments of a photo that had been torn up, but from which she had managed to recover a few scraps. Pieces of silhouettes, simple details that she would then have pasted onto a luminous background.

Her or her memory.

Yes, her memory might well have gone to work that Friday without waiting for her, knowing what it had to do — retain these little fragments for later, when she would be able to put them back together. Or even just to consider them. It could well be that her memory had saved all this for now, for her fortieth birthday.

Four recollections of that day
that her memory had highlighted

It was just a few images.

But her memory had taken care to highlight them, as if it had used some kind of colorless and extremely bright marker pen.

A way of telling her: "They're here, you see? I am looking after them, don't you worry about them. Take care of the rest — for this part of the story, you'll see later. When you're older. In the meantime, I am storing them."

Flavia saw some of these images in motion. Like tiny excerpts from a film that has disappeared or that she can no longer get her hands on.

When the images imposed themselves in this way, they made up sequences of barely a few seconds. But they had one thing in common with the still images Flavia had in her mind, the ones that looked like photographic snapshots: it was as if her memory had carefully tucked them away, tracing a trail of light around them.

"That's probably why we're talking about flashes. All the images that come to me as if they are stuck onto a blinding background correspond to that day, I know it. You know what I mean?"

Yes. I could see exactly what she was talking about, why she could be sure that these images came from that day in December 1984.

It was a matter of intensity, of light. By highlighting them, her memory had authenticated them, as if she had marked them with a luminous rubber stamp. Or as if she had placed them on a radioactive plate.

Those images:

Flavia's father has gone to work, and her mother is asleep. That's why Flavia has gone up to their loft. In this first memory, she sees herself standing in front of her mother who is still in bed, hidden under thick blankets and at least two comforters. Because it is very cold on the morning of that day. For several weeks, the temperatures have been extremely low, not only in Paris, not only in France. "A cold front has hit all of Europe." On TV, the phrase is repeated over and over. In the loft where her parents sleep the air is freezing, even more so than downstairs in the kitchen; moreover, as soon as you open your mouth, your breath freezes into a column of mist. Her mother has covered herself with everything she could find, so that what Flavia has before her eyes does not look like her mother at all, but a shell of fabric and wool under which she can make out the shape of a head.

On the morning of that day, her mother is
    like a huge sleeping tortoise.

Flavia sees herself standing in front of her parents' bed, drumming on the covers as she tries to shake the body underneath: "Mama, wake up. It's time to go to school, Mama. You hear me? You have to take me to school; I'm going to be late. Mama!" That day, she remembers, it takes a long time to wake her mother up. Very long. In her shell, the mother remains motionless while the little girl's words are lost in the white vapor that comes out of her mouth. At one point, Flavia tells herself that her mother won't wake up, that she won't wake up ever again, that she will remain forever buried under the wooly thickness. In this memory, she does not see her brothers. But she hears one of them screaming. It is perhaps the younger of the boys, Boris, whom she still hears screaming on the soundtrack of these images. But she's not sure, maybe it's Sacha. It makes no difference: in her memory, her two brothers always appear together, like twins. Over the image of the mother-tortoise, she hears the cries of one or the other. Or perhaps on the children's floor the voices of her brothers have time to merge into one before the time the cries reach Flavia's ears, as she stood planted in front of her sleeping mother.

*

Then Flavia sees a sequence that fixes itself into a strange image. It was the same day, that of the mother-tortoise — no doubt about it, it's another one of those recollections that her memory has highlighted. This time, Flavia is at school. A head appears behind the glass partition, in the upper part of the door. The head is motionless, almost glued to the glass. It is a strange apparition: Flavia knows that she jumped when she saw it. It's because the head is that of her father. Her father who shouldn't be there. It is neither the place nor the time for parents to be there. For one thing, the bell has not rung, but on top of that, the parents usually wait outside on the sidewalk. Yet, his head is there, on the other side of the door. Suddenly, her father's mouth opens wide, his round eyes become two discs, then all at once they leave his face and disappear. And Flavia no longer sees her father's features. At all. Today, in her memory, after the movement of his bulging eyes, she sees only an oval,

the luminous outline of her father's head,
but without eyes, without a mouth, without a nose.

Without hair, either. Like those silhouettes that sometimes appear in activity books and that you have to complete. But it is not an exercise, or a page torn from a vacation notebook. That image behind the glass is her father. For real. Only, where his face should be, there is nothing. It is perhaps the overly bright glow accompanying this memory that prevents her from discerning his features. By highlighting her father's apparition on the other side of the door, Flavia's memory erased them. His open mouth and the bulging discs of his eyes may still be there, behind that dazzling light. That's it for her second memory.

*

Then there is this other one.

Flavia is still at school. The day is over, all the children have gone home. All the children except her, because that day, the Mistress insisted on keeping her. "You, Flavia, you stay with me." She explains to her that she has to stay after class because she didn't quite understand the math lesson. So they have to go back to one of the morning exercises together, the one where you have to add up candies. In this sequence, the Mistress sits next to her and speaks with her voice so soft and clear, that voice that Flavia still has in her ear. But the Mistress is strange that day. Even if she is speaking in her cool, composed voice, the voice she has always had, in this third memory her face is as if closed. Her eyes especially. It looks like she has covered them with a veil, like on that day, when all the other children are gone and Flavia is alone with her, her eyes aren't as bright as before. She sees it plainly: suddenly, the voice and the eyes of the Mistress no longer go together at all. Is it the math lesson that the Mistress feels obliged to start all over again, just for her, that is putting her in this weird state? Is she angry? Next to the Mistress, that day, Flavia sees herself going over one of the morning exercises. She applies herself, she does her best: she likes her Mistress very much, so she would like to reassure her by showing her that she has understood. Moreover, she gets the set exercise right on the first try: Flavia is sure that the answer in her exercise book is the correct one. But the Mistress refuses to let her go. She says: "Yes, okay, but what if there were a five there?" And a two instead of a three?" With a large eraser, she changes the objects and numbers in Flavia's notebook: five sweets become three dolls, then two tea towels. The Mistress gives her other sums to do, two or three in a row, and she thinks up for her: "other problems," as she says. But the little girl can see that she is basically asking the same thing each time.

"Mistress, is this answer okay? And how about that one?"

The Mistress nods yes, yet she scribbles even more new numbers as her eyes become more and more opaque. That day, her eyes no longer go at all with her soft voice. Behind their veil it even seems that the Mistress's eyes are very concerned. What in the world did Flavia do that she wouldn't be let out of that classroom? Why can't she go home like the other children? It's now so long since the bell rang. They're probably waiting for her on the sidewalk, in front of the school door, in the cold. Is her mother worrying about her? In Paris the air is icy, it stings the nose and ears as soon as you go out onto the street. But Flavia doesn't care about having to brave the cold; she wants to leave this classroom, find her mother and go home, get away from the gaze of the Mistress, from her eyes that are so strange despite her voice that tries to sound as soft as it usually does. "Let's see, Flavia, this other exercise now" ... Flavia gasps, she can't take it anymore, she wants to leave. Even though a cold snap has struck all of Europe, even though the TV says that the temperatures are: "historically low." But the Mistress does not want to let her go. Flavia wants to cry, maybe she's already crying. Then the veil which covered so ineffectively the Mistress's eyes is finally in tatters. And Flavia finds herself faced with a frightened look — two immobile and bewildered blue eyes, as bewildered as those of her father behind the glass, those two discs that had finally disappeared.

"Mistress": that's what she called her, never "Mrs" or "Miss." That's it for the third memory sequence.

*

From the same day, after all that, there is a fourth recollection highlighted in Flavia's memory. These are the last images she has of this Friday in December 1984. This time, Flavia is in a police car, sitting in the back seat. Beside her, the policewoman is not being nice, not nice at all. She is tense and stern, huddled in her uniform, and she doesn't even look at her. Flavia nevertheless dares to ask a question: "Are we going to be on TV?"

Oh, it's not that she wants to be on TV, not at all. Neither her parents nor her brothers: oh no, please don't let them be on TV.

If we go on TV, it'll mean that it's serious.

That's exactly what Flavia thinks to herself. She doesn't want to be in the newspaper. No. Not the newspaper, not the TV. Her eyes burn just thinking about it, she feels her heart beating in the back of her throat, as if it had left her chest to get stuck there, in her throat. No, not the TV!

Let them continue talking about this winter that arrived earlier than expected, about the cold snap that hit the continent, about the port of Cherbourg caught in the ice, let them continue with the frost, the snow and the wind, but please don't talk about us. Oh no, don't talk about what happened to us today! "Are we going to be on TV?" She hears herself asking the question again, but the policewoman still does not answer. Or maybe she did reply. Maybe she had given a response, maybe that cold-faced woman in her uniform had finally said something.

But she doesn't remember anymore: it's because this time, Flavia's memory and its luminous pen had pushed down hard and had really overdone it.

In Flavia's head today, it is like the end of this sequence is incandescent.

Like a piece of film that has been subjected to too much heat, a piece of film that would have finally caught fire. Fourth and final sequence.

GRISELDA

Return to Le Bûcheron; December 2018.
À la Jean Seberg

Shortly after meeting Flavia, I arranged to meet her mother at the same Parisian café, Le Bûcheron.

Both arrived a few minutes after me.

A few weeks apart, I saw them enter Le Bûcheron by the main entrance, the one that opens onto the Rue de Rivoli. They made the same gesture to close the door behind them and came towards my table walking in a similar way.

It wasn't until Griselda was sitting across from me that I noticed that, while I waited for her, I had spontaneously sat down at the same table as when I had arranged to meet her daughter at the beginning of November. At a place where the banquette is abruptly interrupted because there is a slight recess in the wall — which is very practical because in this place, on the banquette side, you can lean back or put your shoulder in the nook. That's why I choose this spot every time I have a meet-up that is likely to last a while, under the portrait of a woman wearing a bun. Just like that, Griselda had sat down in exactly the same place that Flavia had occupied a month and a half earlier, no doubt on the same chair. In any case, it was in the same place in the room, in front of the woman in the painting.

These coincidences troubled me, as did their resemblance. They have the same intense gaze; but while Flavia's hair is shoulder length, Griselda's is extremely short, leaving her ears, temples and forehead entirely bare. À la Jean Seberg, from the time when the actress had her hair cut short, when she was Otto Preminger's

Saint Joan. Except that Griselda's hair is very dark and her eyes are a deep brown, almost black in fact. Her daughter's eyes are almost the same, dark and surprisingly lustreless.

Griselda orders a coffee, says something about her haircut, while stroking the back of her neck: "I like to wear it short, but this time the hairdresser went a bit overboard…" I reassure her, tell her that it suits her. I am sincere and I believe that deep down, she agrees. Griselda smiles.

On her almost bare scalp I try to spot the mark left by a wound that I know exists. The place where a bullet punctured Griselda's skull a long time ago. I would like to ask her questions, but I'm not sure how to go about it, even though I have thought about it a lot in the weeks leading up to our meeting.

Luckily, I don't need to question her. She is much more serene than I imagined; smiling and obviously happy to be there.

From the beginning, Griselda and I spoke in Spanish. In the same way as I had done with her daughter in French — spontaneously, one then the other language came to us. If they were both in front of me at the same time, I wonder which language we would have spoken?

The notebook that I take out of my bag and open immediately on the table between the two of us does not intimidate her at all, quite the contrary, no more so than my book project, about which she does not ask me much. She seems to know that everything will depend on the meetings I am having, in large part on what she wants to tell me, what she wants to help me understand. And on my ability to listen to her.

Am I capable of that?

For her to make sense of things, she has to speak. So, with her coffee before her, without hesitating, she begins to tell the story. And I start taking notes.

December 1984; snow, salt and sand

Griselda remembers.

It was she who had appeared to Flavia as a mother-tortoise. Griselda, whom her daughter could not remove from her shell of cotton and wool, although she shook her in the icy air, drumming on the blankets in the loft space that served as a bedroom for her and Claudio. Yet Flavia would not give up: "Mama, wake up. It's time to go to school, Mama. You hear me? You have to take me to school; I'm going to be late. Mama!" But Griselda couldn't, her head ached horribly, and she couldn't even move her feet. It was a Friday in December 1984 and for several weeks she had been wearing far too much make-up. For months, maybe. Later that day, behind her painted face, in the doorway, she had called Claudio. "I don't feel well, Claudio, come." That day, she had asked him for help. Because that day was strange, that day everything was different.

Griselda remembers that it was incredibly cold and that was all they talked about on TV. Understandably so, as they were entering into: "an historic winter."

Paris suddenly appeared to Griselda as an unfamiliar city. Yet she had been living there for ten years. Ten years since she had fled Argentina to settle in France. But with all this snow that never stopped falling, in this cold, the slightest gesture seemed new to her, and she felt like she had everything to learn. Where do you put your feet on the icy slabs so as not to smash your skull when everything is freezing up around you? When everything gets slippery, hostile, and you don't know what to do?

From her first winter as a caretaker, she had learned that salt helps prevent snow from turning into ice. "Here are the bags of salt," she had been told in the high school where they worked and lived at the same time. She had paused for a moment. So, the person who handed her the bags opened one in front of her before starting to do what she was supposed to do: "With the salt, you have to do it like this, you see." And Griselda had taken over, spreading the salt in the yard and on the sidewalk, in front of the building's main door. Not to mention the entrance to the lodge she occupied with Claudio and little Flavia, who had been born during their first autumn at T. High School. Griselda must not fall. She must not slip when she stood there, as she often did, with her baby in her arms, to look out from the entrance of the lodge at the small garden. Even under the snows of winter the garden looked beautiful to her. "But I must not slip, anyway, I shouldn't fall with the little one" — that's what Griselda had told herself during Flavia's first winter. From the first snow, a few months after the birth of her daughter. That's why when she found out about the salt, she had got into the habit of salting the entryway of their little apartment. Of the lodge that served as their apartment.

Covered with salt, the snow became very soft then disappeared little by little as the fine white layer that covered the courtyard was pierced with translucent puddles. This salt trick worked very well, that's why each winter the arrival of the bags of salt reassured Griselda. Like the umbrella that you slip into the bottom of your bag because storms have been forecast. Like the net that the acrobat sees under his feet, just before launching himself. Whenever there was a chance of snow or just frost, Griselda put her fingers on the salt bags and she felt calmer.

But this time it was different. The snow had been much heavier than usual. Like every time it snowed, Griselda and Claudio had salted the yard; working together it was done quickly. Each had their own half, each their own territory, until they met in line with the gate that led into their little garden. However, this time that had not been enough. Claudio had had to clear the snow with a big shovel they had been given.

But the following week it had snowed again, really heavily.

So, the same person who had taught them about the salt came and told them: "This year it's too cold, the salt won't be enough." And she handed them sandbags.

That's how Griselda had learned about the sand.

This time, she hadn't needed any explanations, she had immediately spread the sand in the yard and in front of the sidewalk, like an experienced janitor. On her half of the yard, at least. Claudio had done the same on the other half. They had met up very quickly in front of the little garden surrounded by a railing, like those you see in the squares that are everywhere in Paris, except that this square was just for them. Then Griselda had insisted on spreading a few more handfuls in front of the entrance to the lodge. Their home was small now that there were five of them, but they had become used to it. She had spread sand on the flagstones in front of the entrance, then she had thrown a large handful of it on the doorstep. A very large handful, just for the doorstep.

She did that as the boys would not stop sliding everywhere. Even when they stood in the doorway watching her work in the yard. Even when they looked as if they were behaving themselves.

Boris and Sacha had no reason to leave the house. "Stay there, be good," she told them all the time. "There's too much snow, it's too cold." Since the beginning of December, the courtyard had become an ice rink: *No salgan, chicos, no se muevan*, she kept saying. Griselda kept Boris and Sacha at home, they didn't have to go outside. For Flavia it was different. She had to cross the street since she was in preparatory class in the school just across the road. The little ones, on the other hand, could stay in the lodge, which did not stop their mother from always keeping an eye on them. For her to be able to watch them, all they had to do was stay on the doorstep, given that for Griselda more or less everything happened there, in the now, white school courtyard.

But at three and four years old, boys are like mad dogs.

They push and jostle each other and seeing each other fall makes them burst out laughing. It was rare for them to just sit there and behave well. That cold excited them in a strange way, along with all that snow that kept freezing, hardening and essentially becoming something else. "Keep still, stop fidgeting!" she called to them from the yard. The boys smiled broadly to show they had understood, seemingly staying in the doorway. But even clinging to the frame, Boris and Sacha slipped. While hanging on to each other, their feet searched for a corner of icy slab and they always found a way to end up on their backsides. "Stop! You're going to hurt yourselves!" protested Griselda. But the more the boys fell, the more they laughed.

That's why she had insisted on salting the doorway. A big handful of salt, then an even bigger handful of sand, to prevent the boys from hurting themselves, even if Griselda knew full well that it would not be enough.

The lodge and the garden

She and her husband had been working for a little over six years as caretakers and handypersons at T. High School, a private establishment in eastern Paris. It was Father Adur who found them this job shortly before Flavia was born. Adur was a revolutionary priest, an Assumptionist and yet left-wing. An Argentine exile, like them. It was he who had married them in the school chapel long before they did so at the town hall, at the bottom of this courtyard that she had known without snow, without salt and without sand. Since Father Adur had found them this job, most of their lives had been spent there, within the walls of the establishment.

She was so heavily pregnant when they moved into the lodge at T. High School in the late summer of 1978. She still sees herself — how strange and comical she was when she thinks about it. When Father Adur had married them in the little chapel, she had already entered her eighth month of pregnancy.

Flavia was born, then two more pregnancies followed. Twice again, she had seen her belly grow between the lodge, the dustbin room, and the roses to be pruned once the students had left. She recalls that when she could feel a foot, an elbow and a knee of whoever was inside she knew the pregnancy was coming to an end. That when her tummy, which had become too small for the person it contained, contorted to resemble a big lumpy quince she knew that it would soon be over, that very soon she would give birth. That's how after Flavia, there was Sacha then Boris. Since the priest had helped them get into the building, their whole life had taken place within the walls of T. High School. It was there that Claudio and Griselda loved each other. Where things went wrong, sometimes. Where three children had grown inside her. There, too, Claudio would occasionally push her about, after the premises had emptied, the children had fallen asleep, when everything around became silent. She never really knew how that started. Anger suddenly rose in him without his understanding why, that's what he always told her the next day. You see, afterwards he felt bad. If it was rose season, he would make a bouquet just for her, trying to arrange them nicely in a container that he placed in the center of the table, then he would begin to peel the vegetables to prepare for dinner. Coming back from the courtyard, when she saw flowers and Claudio from behind, busy at the sink, a peeler in his hand, she knew that he was sorry for the day before.

It all happened there. Between their small apartment overlooking the school courtyard and the miniature garden that had convinced them to accept the job. Like a little square, really, and just for them, too. How could they refuse: everyone dreams of having a garden of their own.

Their life took place there until December 1984.

Until this sudden and so unusual coldness.

Fuel oil or heating oil

Griselda remembers.

The boiler had been working at full power for several weeks already. It was an oil-fired boiler that was generally fueled during school holidays. But this time it wasn't going to be enough. So, the person who gave them the bags of salt every year, the same person who this time had also supplied them with the bags of sand, had come to tell them that two days later a truck would come to fill up the boiler, a little earlier than scheduled. "They're going to make a new fuel delivery; it can't wait for the Christmas holidays. The truck will come very early in the morning, before the first teaching period." Claudio and Griselda had to be ready to meet the tanker, around seven o'clock.

"But what about the fuel oil, the *mazout*, then?" Griselda had asked.

The man had stood looking at her for a moment, not understanding her. She told herself that once again she must have mispronounced the word. "The *mazout*, what about the oil?" She repeated the question, gritting her teeth as she vibrated her tongue against her palate, concentrating on that French "z" she had trouble pronouncing. That was probably why the man had looked at her, staring at her make-up, as if forbidden to do so. So, the second time she had made a real effort, she had done her best and it had worked rather well since she had a tickling sensation on her palate. But after the awkward silence she was accustomed to whenever the person she was talking to didn't understand her, the man shrugged his shoulders before bursting out laughing: "Fuel oil or heating oil, it is the same thing! The truck will arrive around seven o'clock to deliver fuel oil… Or heating oil if you prefer… It's all the same… The same thing, you understand?" Suddenly, the man had begun to speak really loudly, as if she were deaf, with big hand gestures as if he had to be a mime artist to get this woman standing before him to understand, and she could feel herself reddening with embarrassment. "Okay, yes, yes, okay… Fuel oil or heating oil, it's the same thing," Griselda had repeated to let him know that she had understood; no need to go on. Then she had shaken her head, herself amused by the question she'd asked: "Fuel oil or heating oil, of course," as if she had always known that, really. As if she were both this overly made-up foreigner who, every year, from the first frosts, had everything to learn — salt then sand, heating oil and fuel oil. And this man, there in front of her, who found her a little stubborn and clumsy: "but hey, basically, she's very nice, the janitor, she comes from the end of the world, what you gonna do? Sometimes she looks at you with her big black eyes that widen because she doesn't understand what you say to her, she opens her eyes wide for really silly things, sometimes, things you don't expect"... Griselda knew that the man in front of her, that very evening, would say that about her, that he had already said it plenty of times, no doubt, she had so often given him the opportunity to do so. Upon their arrival at the end of the summer of 1978, and still today. As if all those years spent in the high school had been for nothing, as if she had never stopped repeating a year, as a caretaker. Then she laughed at herself. And suddenly she was both of those people. The janitor with glittery eyelids who doesn't know anything, the janitor who has a headache and really doesn't understand a single thing. And the person surprised and softened by the janitor's ignorance. "She's not from here, what do you expect...?"

It was because of this fuel oil episode that a few days before that Friday in December 1984 Claudio and Griselda woke up well before their usual time. To greet the tanker, all because of this historic coldness. So, she had come down from their loft backwards, in the dark, clinging to the ladder, searching with her toes for the rungs that she had no trouble finding. She had come to know this lodge by heart. The smallest corner. Even the gaps between the rungs of the ladder, the one that gave access to their loft and the other one too, where the children were. Claudio had cut some planks and then he had put together the two lofts, all by himself. Without that, how could they have lived with five people in there?

On the morning of the fuel oil, that was also the morning of the heating oil, the three children were still asleep. It was almost winter and at seven o'clock in the morning, daybreak was still far away. What temperature could it be outside? Minus ten, minus eleven degrees? The day before, they had talked about it on the 'Antenne 2' news show: it had been a long time since it had been so cold in Paris. On TV, they had talked about the winter of 1956 and even that of 1880. Everyone who had known the winter of 1880 was already dead and buried, but in France there are records for everything, so they could still talk about the winter of 1880. Here, time flows differently than in the Americas. Thirty years earlier, one hundred and twelve, two hundred and three or four hundred and fifty-nine years, they can measure time with big shovelfuls, and still no one is lost, everyone finds their way. So, the TV reporter was able to compare, quite pleased with himself: "It's almost as cold as it was in 1880."

And then there was the Thursday before that day.

Griselda had gone out into the yard well before seven o'clock to start clearing the snow that had fallen in the night, in front of the door of the lodge and the one that had been built into the railing that surrounded their little garden. She had spread salt and then sand around her. Claudio had then joined her with this huge shovel that he dug into the powdery snow.

She was very tired; she remembers that very well. In the yard made silent by the snow her boots sank into the ground making a strange noise, a muffled noise that nevertheless echoed inside her.

It was the first time she had walked in such deep snow, and under her feet it sounded like someone had turned a sock inside out or something, a cracking perceived from within. It was morning and it was night. Griselda moved through the night and did not recognize her footsteps. This whole story of fuel oil delivered well before dawn had tired her so much.

It does seem to her that on this Thursday, at some point, she and Claudio had argued a lot. So, before going to bed, she had probably taken something to help her sleep.

Doubled the dose, maybe.

It helps, all that, it soothes, it feels good, funnily, too, it allows you to forget a lot of things. Perhaps she hadn't measured what she had swallowed the day before that day.

Or maybe not. When she thinks about it, she tells herself that she had taken nothing out of the ordinary. That if that morning she had so much trouble getting up, it was just because her head ached. Unless the explanation lies elsewhere.

Whatever was going on inside her, no doubt did not want her to wake up.

On the morning of that day, she had had such a hard time getting out of bed.

But she remembers that a little later, she still found the strength to put on her make-up.

For weeks, perhaps months, she had had a passion for make-up. There was always someone ready to point it out to her. "Griselda, you wear too much make-up."

'Pfft,' she didn't care. She felt like it calmed her down. Pencils, lipsticks, blushes, creams. Glitter. You can do incredible things with it, hide everything, change everything. She sat down in front of the mirror, she applied to her face everything she could get her hands on, and immediately she felt better. Sometimes she spent hours there.

That day, she had done her make-up for a long time in front of the mirror.

Until the point when all she saw in the mirror before her was a mass of colors.

It is perhaps there, before this image, that she broke.

The children must have been playing at her feet. Yes, maybe the two boys were playing at her feet.

Suddenly, Griselda got up, crossed the snowy courtyard, and

went to look for Claudio in the classroom he was repainting.

It's weird, now that she thinks about it. For him, too, colors were his thing. He adored that. He has always loved that.

But that day, for her, it was different.

On her face, the colors no longer soothed her. On the contrary, they made her feel really bad.

This is what she had wanted to explain to him, in the doorway: *No me siento bien*. But Claudio had sent her packing.

Griselda feels that she has to tell me all of that.

Even if it doesn't really explain anything.

Because who could explain what happened that day?

That's how Griselda sometimes refers to it: *what happened.*

That day, before what happened, she had wanted to forget herself in the colors, but she entered into the night.

And the night, after that day, never left her again.

La Plata, 1974.
Like in a Kalatozov movie

Griselda wanted to talk to me about that day in December 1984. But before that, she had things to tell me. It was important, she had to talk about it.

So, Griselda began to go back in time, to pick up the thread of her memory for me, in reverse.

As I listened to her, I kept taking notes under the severe portrait painting.

After the "historic" Parisian cold, Griselda reminisced about meeting Claudio in a bookshop. In Argentina, this time, in La Plata. It was in 1974.

She knew I could mentally picture the scene, so she gave more details:

"The bookshop was called 'Libraco', and to be precise it was on Calle 6, between 45 and 46."

I didn't need more information: as soon as Griselda gave me this precise address, I located the place on the grid map of La Plata. The city map looks like those grids that you use to play battleships. As soon as you give an address to a resident of La Plata or to a person who has visited the city a little, they sketch a cross in their head on the drawing that every insider forever keeps in their memory. A plan that's something of a game board or a target, when you think about it: a five-by-five-kilometer square, or twenty-five square kilometers altogether, made up of thirty-eight by thirty-eight city blocks. Almost always square and pierced by several diagonals, including two main ones that cross the city from side to side and intersect in its geometric center. Plaza Moreno is in the middle of the target, precisely where diagonal 73, drawn from east to west, meets diagonal 74, which crosses La Plata from north to south. From that point, the geometric obsession spreads out in all directions, impossible to escape: if you go towards the north, the south, the east or the west, on all of the six roads you will find an avenue, and at the intersection of two avenues, you will always find a square. It's like this:

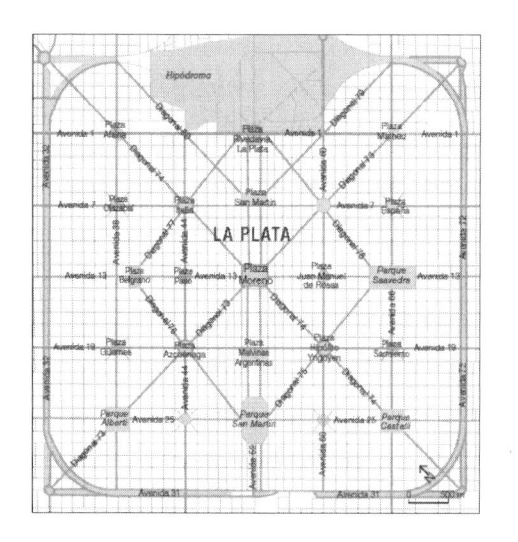

As for them, they met each other near to the Plaza Italia.

Claudio always went to the bookshop with his elder son. He lived with a woman and had two boys, Sylvain 8 and Damien 10, she had heard said. But when she saw him, it was generally with the elder boy. People said that the mother of the children was a Frenchwoman whom Claudio had met a few years earlier in Cuba: "You could not miss her in La Plata, she has one of those accents…" It's sometimes other people who happen to have accents, when you think about it now, Griselda smiles. It was said that Claudio had met the mother of his children during a trip, the story of which ended up seducing Griselda, a story of revolution, prison, guns and new times. The kind of adventures that we necessarily spoke of in a low voice, which added to the charm of the whole thing. Besides, he had started with the guns even earlier, well before the Cuban Revolution. "Well you see, he was right there from the beginning of the Peronist resistance of 1955, even on June 9, 1956, he was in the area. He's known as the 'White Wolf' and well-respected, he's not just anyone, not some hanger-on," was what a friend who she had confided in had told her. It was through listening to others talk about him that Griselda had fallen madly in love with Claudio: it seemed to her that this tall, dark-haired, bespectacled man was some sort of hero, a character straight out of Rodolfo Walsh's *Operation Massacre*. "But be careful who you talk to about him, you shouldn't put him in danger, your Claudio."

When she had learned all that, she had not yet spoken a single word to "her" Claudio. What happened between them had no need for words.

In any case, at that time, she did not know he was married. Father, okay, but married, she didn't know, they had no doubt forgotten to tell her. In truth, she had not tried too hard to find out. Deep down, she knew it didn't matter. He was hanging around her and she already loved him, that was all.

Claudio was handsome. Very. And he still is, at eighty-seven, with his white hair and his khaki-green trousers, as if for him time had stopped when he was doing his guerrilla training in El Escambray, somewhere in the vicinity of Cienfuegos.

It is very important to picture this bookshop, on Calle 6, between 45 and 46. It's simple, if this place had not existed, none of this would have happened. First, Griselda could not have carried on. And when she says that she is not even thinking about her meeting with Claudio. Without this place, she couldn't have continued: couldn't have, really, without something or someone to get her through. Couldn't have, at all. She needed to push the door of the bookshop to keep going.

She remembers how she would rush to her hangout spot in the evening, after work, to see if Claudio was there, too. He would be there, for sure: that's what she told herself on the way, though the fear that he might not be gave her a knot in her stomach. But he was always there and as soon as she saw him, her anxiety disappeared.

All she had to do was push the door of the bookshop to fall unfailingly onto him, watching the entrance from the back of the shop. They hadn't arranged to meet, and yet he was obviously expecting her. Slowly, Griselda closed the door behind her, she looked up and fell on Claudio's delighted smile. So, she had come. When she thinks about it today, she says it was like a movie. As beautiful as the reunion scenes in those Russian films she loved so much. All it took was for her to push open the door of the bookshop and bump into Claudio for her to become the heroine of a film by Kalatozov.

They didn't talk to each other. That's what made what happened after magical. From the first time they saw each other, they came together in a perfectly silent game, a game with rules they seemed to have known forever.

After pushing open the bookshop door, she headed towards the back of the room as if she knew the book she was looking for and where to find it. Without hesitating, she took a few steps, stopped in front of a shelf and grabbed a book that she immediately opened, right in the middle, before her eyes stopped at a place on the page she had before her, as if she were just continuing a reading that had been momentarily interrupted. Claudio then came to her side, pretending to read over her shoulder, like he was resuming the suspended reading with her. But neither of them read.

It was so beautiful and strange, she remembers, and from then on things always happened the same way.

All he had to do was brush against her for her breathing to stop suddenly. He realized it, suddenly her breath was suspended, her lips opened by themselves — but not to breathe, no, since she was in a kind of apnea. She felt her lips pull apart. But there was nothing between them, not even a wisp of air. It was weird that everything stopped like that, that there was only his presence. Neither the people around, nor the voices or the book. She had tried to reproduce this feeling, alone, at home: where everything suddenly disappears, even the air around her, and for a moment there would be nothing but her parted lips. But it was impossible. The way her breath would stop, this time outside of time: Claudio had to be there, beside her, for these wonders to take place.

Then Claudio smiled from up high. He was so much taller than her. A tall, slender, short-sighted man.

For her part, after his smile, Griselda seemed to pull herself together. She closed the book, took a few more steps and their game began again. A few minutes had passed and now he was close to her again. She didn't have to turn to see him to know he was standing there, just inches away. The very thought of this closeness made her breath stop again. For him, it was the exact opposite. She had already noticed it at the time, she would confirm it later: desire made his nostrils swell, they emptied and filled with air more and more quickly as if, just like that, he was starting to breathe for two. It was in La Plata that she had made this discovery: when Claudio desired her, his nostrils began to beat above her forehead like the heart of a breathless animal.

At the other end of the shop, the bookseller followed their dance.

From the time their paths had crossed, from their first moments, things between them had been like this. Every time they saw each other they resumed their game.

But even before Claudio this place had started to mean a lot. Calle 6, between 45 and 46, she would never forget that place. Those she came across there; all those chairs occupied by people with an open book on their lap. Or not, just to be there, like her. To escape the outside world. Everyone else locked out. And outside, it was not desire that prevented people breathing. Outside, they were suffocating for real. Griselda was suffocating for real.

Maybe not as much as when she was still living with her parents. But still. When she met Claudio, she had been working for several years as a librarian at the University of La Plata and living alone. She had a good salary, at least twice that earned by most people she knew. With that money, she wanted for nothing and with help from her father to buy a small apartment, Griselda had been able to buy her independence. But that didn't stop her from suffocating.

Outside was asphyxiation.

The city, Argentine society, the continent. Asphyxiation.

But for me to understand all this, she had to go back before 1974 and take another leap in time. More than twenty years back.

Griselda then paused, she turned to the waiter.

"I would like another coffee. You too, right?"

While waiting for our next two coffees to arrive, I leafed through the notebook I had taken just for her story. I had already filled a good ten pages with blue ink.

La MADRE and her so blonde doll

Griselda then told me about her childhood in the countryside, in the south of the province of Buenos Aires where her parents had settled after their marriage and the births of their children.

After the birth of their fourth child, in fact. It was only after the arrival of the last, a pretty blonde with blue eyes, that her parents decided to leave town. As if after the little something had been accomplished, it was something else worthy of marking the occasion. She was so blonde, everyone was ecstatic, *que hermosa, te salió rubia, Mabel, tan rubia, tan blanca de piel, como una muñeca de porcelana*, very white-skinned, as in the tales that she had been read so many times, very fair-skinned and so blonde, like the beautiful princesses of old.

Yes, now that she thinks back, that's exactly it: it was only after the birth of her little sister that her parents felt the need for the great outdoors, for a huge garden all to themselves. The family had then left La Plata to go to a backwater where her father had opened a pharmacy. Because he was a pharmacist, the father: "That's important, my father was a pharmacist," Griselda insisted, suddenly, and in my notebook, I underlined it: pharmacist.

So, her pharmacist father had thought that it would be easier to make his business prosper in the middle of the countryside than in La Plata where the children had been born. There, he would have no competition.

But the word makes you smile when you know the place.

They lived in a house with an immense courtyard that extended into the countryside all around, the pampas that was never ending and that had immediately become her own landscape, like an extension of the house. Her territory was infinite. All this happened near Monte Hermoso, not far from Punta Alta, in the middle of nowhere. The sea was not far away, but they never saw it. The nearest town was fifty kilometers away.

There were four children: Griselda and her twin brother were the "middle" children, caught between the eldest — the pampered child, the boy they had so wanted — and the youngest, the porcelain doll, the apple of her mother's eye. *¡Que linda!* It was because she was so beautiful, the little one: "You would think she was from Sweden. That translucent skin, those eyes so blue…" Everyone was ecstatic. Each time she had the youngest one in her arms, the mother smiled, pleased with herself — *Sí, la última me* *salió rubia*. The youngest was a blessing for the mother: "Four children are tiring, no two ways about it. But you were right to have that one. She is so cute. How right you were to have her." She and her twin were sandwiched between the other two, the eldest: "so big, so strong, a handsome lad, and so smart." And the doll. So blonde, so sweet.

Sandwiched, that's what the twins were: they were the thing between the two pieces of bread, the thing you don't see, the thing that sweats away in between. She remembers her certainty of being unloved — her twin, she doesn't know how he felt, but she had no doubts about it. She had hair as black as her eyes, thick and even darker eyebrows, so when they saw Griselda next to her little sister, the women would say: "Look at that, your two daughters, they are like day and night."

She was the night.

It made her laugh, more than anything.

"You're the night yourself, you crazy old woman," was what she had said to herself the first time she had heard it. Really, deep down, it made her laugh. Or maybe not, now that she thinks about it. Perhaps Griselda ended up laughing about it. But at six years old, no. In fact, it hadn't made her laugh at all the first time the neighbor had said it, while her mother strutted around with the princess in her arms, her princess, so proud to have that little one.

Maybe it had actually hurt her a lot.

Yes, she remembers now. The first time the neighbor had said: "The two girls, they are like day and night," in her bed that night, Griselda had cried.

Her mother didn't like her. Her father, on the other hand, adored her, Griselda knew that. But the mother kept him from showing it too much. The mother was bad love.

La MADRE.

Now with her coffee in hand, she laughs. But damn, going back in time like that... everything comes back to her, intact. La MADRE, she must have really pissed her off, anyway, La MADRE, damn... The father, he loved her enough for two, she knew it, she has always known it. But La MADRE was like a shield behind which the father always stood.

"Ah, I wish I was that horse"

Luckily, the countryside was there, all around. This unspoilt nature, this Argentine countryside which has nothing to do with what they mean in Europe by countryside. Because in Europe, it's really a joke so far as Griselda was concerned, the countryside is not that at all. It is however very beautiful in Europe; it is not a matter of beauty. It's very beautiful here, isn't it? Soothing like a large, shared garden. So reassuring, basically, because it comes oddly neat, their garden, spruced up, transformed by centuries of human presence, all you have to do is curl up in it and start to purr. It's so different there, isn't it? There, nature arrives without a safety net. It makes you dizzy, it unsettles, it intoxicates, it makes you lose your footing. And Griselda adored that.

She still sees herself running until she was out of breath. If she had had the strength, she could have run for days and in all directions without encountering a single obstacle shaped by human hand. Just grass, lots of grass, the occasional cluster of trees, a few rocks and a stream. At most, you would see the carcass of a dead hare.

Virgin, everything was untouched and new, just for her.

It is said that in the time of the Spaniards, these lands had been divided among a handful of settlers who were told: "Your domain will go to the place where your horse will stop running, gallop, gallop straight ahead, the land will be yours until wherever it stops, until the point, somewhere over there, at the end of the horizon, where your horse will collapse, mortally exhausted. She doesn't know if that's true, but whatever. At night, in her bed, more than once she had said to herself: "Ah, I wish I had been that horse." If La MADRE had let her, she would have run as far as a Spanish horse. As far and as fast as a horse.

She and her twin were happy together.

Deep down, they didn't care about that sandwich thing.

Griselda, in any case, for sure, she didn't give a shit. This is what she thought when she looked at La MADRE: "The shiny thing between two slices of bread, you know what it tells you, the shiny thing between the two slices of bread?" Then she ran off, the horse was going to breathe outside.

To breathe, just that.

A happy childhood, when all is said and done. Despite her bitch of a mother.

The neighbors, the flesh panties and: "ese hijo de puta de Don Valerio"

But then there was the neighbor. The neighbors, in fact. In her memory, today, they merge into one. The cold hands Griselda remembers so well and still feels on her buttocks sometimes, whose were they, Pepe's or Don Valerio's? One of the two had hotter and more calloused palms, drier also. For the other the skin covering the hands was invariably soft and ice cold.

Griselda may have swum against the tide, gotten all the way up there, in time, to tell me all about it and for me to take notes in my notebook. She may have stirred up, dived over and again into the river of her memory, found herself once more in that time. She may have gone back there, really, as if things were happening again, there, at the very moment — today, on this day in December 2018, at Le Bûcheron, opposite the Saint-Paul metro station, sitting with her coffee in front of her. She may have found herself over there at the same time, near Monte Hermoso, when she was four, maybe five years old, in 1946 or 1947. She may have been back there once again, but despite all that the connection between the hands and names had been broken.

She remembers the hands; she still feels them on her buttocks. But for all that she remembers, she does not know whose hands they were.

In any case, Griselda knew that if she went over to Pepe's and he was alone, he would take the opportunity to pull down her panties and caress her buttocks. That's right, she wouldn't fall into his trap, she would be in for it if she did! Even if she didn't go that way but bumped into him alone in the middle of the pampas. Because even in the pampas, you can meet people unexpectedly. Even deep in Patagonia, if she ever ran that far one day, Griselda knew there could be someone, hiding behind a tree. And if that were the case, the man would approach her, he would pretend to have a question to ask her, like Pepe and don Valerio did, to have something to show her — "Here, look" — then he would manage to pull her panties down. Just to see, then to caress her a little. His warm, rough hand on her ass. Or his soft, white hand. No matter. What is certain is that after the caresses on the buttocks, he would slide his hand forward, as Pepe always did, catching her between the thighs and even lifting her slightly. As if after having lowered her panties, he was putting on a new pair, but this time the panties were twisting, wriggling flesh. The thing is she still sees the tips of his fingers fidgeting and rummaging all the way down. But Pepe never dug his fingers into her, it seems to her a good thing that he didn't dig them into her. Nor had

Don Valerio.

Unless Griselda had forgotten about it.

Yes, that could well be the truth.

In any case, one day, her father had punched one or the other of them. She had not seen him do it, but she had heard him say it. It seems to her that it was don Valerio who was punched: "*ese hijo de puta de Don Valerio,*" it seems to her that she herself heard her father saying so to La MADRE, teeth and fists clenched. Yet her father never cursed, and he was not in the habit of hitting people. No doubt he had learned about the lowered panties, that he had seen something or had had a hunch, who knows. Don Valerio's cold, white and soft hand, or dry and rough in places like sandpaper. Slightly lifting her off the ground. Because after having lowered her panties, both men liked to weigh her with one hand, as one does before cutting in two a large summer fruit — a honeydew, a watermelon. She no longer knew which hands went with which neighbor, but no matter, her father had found out. And it was enough for him to crack the jaw of one of them for them both to stop together, at the same time. After this phrase from the father: "*ese hijo de puta de Don Valerio,*" all that had stopped, after this episode neither of them had dared start it up again. After the fist in the face, they had really left her alone, neither of them had dared try it again.

Or maybe Griselda has forgotten if they did.

Anyway, soon after, they left the countryside and went back to La Plata. No more hands, fingers wiggling between her legs like big earthworms, flesh underwear and fruits that you hold in your hands before cutting them in two.

It was the father who had wanted them to return to La Plata where the now grown children would be able to pursue an education: "worthy of the name," as he said.

Griselda remembers this departure, this tearing apart, as a first exile. A rupture.

More than two hours had passed since she had appeared at the Rue de Rivoli and we were still at Le Bûcheron.

Griselda talked and talked some more, her memories rushed back and the pages of my notebook filled up.

No more leaps backward, now Griselda was following the passage of time.

At one point the waitress started setting the tables for dinner. I was afraid that she would interrupt us, as often happens in Parisian cafés, that she would decide it was time for the afternoon customers to leave the place unless they ordered something else. Seeing the waitress bustling about, I expected to hear the phrase that sent you on your way: "Sorry, but it's time to change the service…," and that she would arrive with a menu or a board with the dish and dessert of the day written in chalk. I also expected Griselda would quit telling her story, that she would come out of it, that what she was passing on to me with an unexpected intensity would stop suddenly.

But no: while setting the tables around us, the waitress stood at a distance as if, before our two now empty and cold cups, under the portrait of the woman with the bun, we were installed inside an unbreachable bubble. It was as if Griselda was carried away by her own story. She spoke very quickly in Spanish. I listened to her with my eyes riveted on my notebook, taking all the notes I could while the waitress did what she had to do, respecting what was going on at our table.

The war with La MADRE

It was on their family's return to La Plata that Griselda and her twin entered adolescence.

It had been like a first exile, a first rupture, yes.

Everything had suddenly become so constrained. When she thinks about it, she tells herself that her feeling of asphyxiation goes back to that time. This feeling that she sometimes had that she was suffocating, literally.

Because suddenly the horizon had been replaced by her mother. There, before her eyes: La MADRE. This mother who didn't love her, who had never loved her, in any case since she had had her porcelain doll, the child whom she had all to herself all day. In the small apartment in the city center where they now lived, it was impossible to avoid La MADRE. Griselda always bumped into her, in their little hallway; coming out of the small bathroom, she constantly found herself face to face with La MADRE. Even when she was working away with her back turned, in front of the little sink, in the little kitchen, scrubbing the little faucet. Or when she closed the doors of the dresser because she had just rubbed the silver cockerel with her little cloth. Ever since they had left the countryside, everything had suddenly become small. And in this constrained setting, the lack of love from La MADRE was still just as great. Her sense of the infinite suddenly related no longer in the countryside, but to her mother's coldness. The non-love of La MADRE overflowed everywhere.

And that's why, in the apartment in La Plata, being the thing in the middle of the sandwich, she could no longer give a shit. She was dying in there. She doesn't know if her twin felt like that, but she certainly did. The whole thing was killing her.

Soon the desire to flee, to run away, had turned into an urgent need. Since she had been suffocating in their apartment, she had the impression of having become this Spanish horse able to travel for miles effortlessly. She had always dreamed of being this tireless horse, overflowing with energy and ready to conquer the earth to offer it to whoever would ride the horse. But La MADRE had tied up the horse, so Griselda was enraged, she was going mad over it. Both at home and in high school. Because those were her high school years. That's why they had come back to La Plata, so that she and her two brothers could go to high school.

Griselda felt like punching the walls with her fists, kicking the doors, rushing at La MADRE.

At the time, she found solace in the cinema.

Russian cinema, above all, *War and Peace* by Bondarchuk, she remembers, she had the impression that those images more than the others helped her to breathe, perhaps because of those vast spaces that they have over there. On the screen, the big sky of Russia always seemed strangely familiar to her, it looked like the one she missed so much. All it took was for it to appear for her to see herself under that sky and start to feel better. But in the movie theater the lights always ended up coming on, and the screen fading out. And her sky disappearing. All that remained was to return home and to the war with La MADRE. No peace in this story, only war, real war. Since the family had returned to La Plata, there had been open warfare between her and La MADRE.

She remembers clearly: at the time, she worshiped Simone de Beauvoir, and *The Second Sex* above all, a book she had read and then immediately placed on the shelf above her bed. So that La MADRE would see it. Because she knew that this book was driving her mad. She went completely crazy, La MADRE, as soon as she saw the back of the book. As if the mere sight of it assailed her, as if Beauvoir had spat in her face. "Stop with that," La MADRE would say every time she saw the book, "stop with that, Griselda!" Then La MADRE grabbed the book, digging her nails into the cover, she wanted to take it away from there, snatch the book from the shelf above her daughter's bed (the daughter, yes of course, the other one would never put such a horror above their bed, day and night, I can tell you) as if it had been a leech from which she had to be freed, a tick, a bug, a louse. But Griselda immediately threw herself at La MADRE, she seized the book and held it close to her. That book wasn't a leech, it was her treasure, the apple of her eye: "Don't touch it, don't touch Simone, you understand, go away, get out of my room!" Then La MADRE would start screaming: "But you're going to end up being a tramp, I tell you, a poor lost girl, ¡una puta!"

At the other end of the girls' room, in her always perfectly made white bed, her pure blonde sister was watching them. Even when she sat up in bed, her sister's sheets remained smooth, never creased. Her sister was delicate, tidy, pretty, polite, graceful, "so feminine already," her mother said, smiling. Always well groomed. The nails of her fine fingers were never dirty. She never gnawed on them. Fingers of a harpist, a pianist, fairy-like fingers. With mother-of-pearl nails. Her sister. A princess, like in the fairy tales. "Like day and night, those two," it was true, Griselda could see it clearly.

Then she would scream.

Sick of the sandwich

La MADRE did not like Griselda. She had never liked her, but since the whole family had returned to La Plata, Griselda saw only that and thought about it all the time. She and her twin had come too soon after the perfect eldest sibling. She had heard it one day. An aunt or a neighbor, she no longer knew which, had spoken these words. Unless she had imagined it: "They came too soon, those two, that's why you're so tired, take it easy."

One day she felt like throwing the phrase in her face, launching it at La MADRE, like that, at the table, in the middle of a meal. "We came too early, huh?" Her father was beside her, he immediately put his hand on her shoulder: "What are you saying, Griselda, what's up with you?" It was the meat on her plate that had brought it to her mind. Because of this whole thing about the sandwich, the sandwiched twins. She had seen the meat on her plate, and she had suddenly wanted to vomit, to puke all over La MADRE. "And two for the price of one, bonus, two for the price of one, the sandwich filling — double steak!" Then she tossed her piece of meat across the room. Curiously, La MADRE had reacted gently, trying to calm her down.

"But what are you saying, Griselda, my family is the dearest thing to me... How can you say you came too soon? Tell us! I am a woman, a mother..."

"A wife, a mother! Do you hear that? A wife, a mother, but what do you mean? And that's what you want to make us pay for, right? A wife, a mother? But no one forced you to... A wife, a mother, you really didn't have to, you know. You weren't obliged, not at all!"

"But what are you saying, Griselda? My darling, what's wrong with you?"

"Oh, don't touch me, don't touch me, don't give me any of your bullshit... You think that's what you are, fucking hell, a wife, a mother, no, anything but..."

She remembers the anger, the rage that sometimes gripped her in the stomach. But it's not a metaphor, you understand? No, it's something real: there, in the gut. And in the throat, too.

Eventually calm returned. There was always a moment when La MADRE took on an air of sweetness and whispered in her ear the good resolutions she might make, like these doubles disguised as cherubs that you see whispering in the ears of Tex Avery characters: "Teacher, that would be good for you. It's always good for a woman, to be a teacher. Teaching, as I did before I had you. Later, when you get married, later, when you have children, even if you stop working, what you have learned will serve you. With your family."

When she harped on again about this whole teacher thing, it was rage that suddenly rose up in Griselda's head. It really did rise up. A ball of fire: from the gut to the throat, throat to head, rage shattering everything in its path. It bustled, no — that word is not enough. This rage bursts from the depths of the entrails. Then it breaks, tears up everything in its path, this rage leaves the skin raw. Wherever this rage has passed, afterwards everything is left in blood. This rage is like a horse gone mad. For some time, the Spanish horse she had dreamed of had passed inside of her, it had entered her.

Yes, that's exactly it. The horse had moved inside of her.

Drawing

Then Griselda began to draw. A lot, in fact. She had always loved drawing, but suddenly it was different. Suddenly she understood that it was very important. One morning, she had taken a notebook, then she had drawn. Landscapes, heads, horses, silhouettes, profiles, knees, hands. For hours. In one go, with a black pencil that was lying around, she had covered almost half of a notebook. Images came to her by the dozen. A foot, the nape of a neck, an eye, nothing but the iris — then the rump of a horse. Fingers, in various positions. Fingers that grip, pinch, caress, tremble. She discovered that she could draw anything, even sweat and tremors, even anger. Everything. It did her a lot of good, she remembers, to see all these images coming out of her and cover the pages of this notebook, it did her a world of good. Around, people were happy. The boys had come to see, her twin and the eldest admired her work. Even her little sister had come over, she would turn the pages of the notebook before pointing to the drawing she liked most. Even La MADRE was pleased with Griselda. "When she draws, she's calmer," the father said.

So, Griselda had asked for felt-tip pens, and she had been given felt-tip pens, then Griselda had asked for gouaches, and she had been given gouaches. She drew every day after coming home from school. Before dinner, after dinner. Long after dinner. "It's time for lights off, you're getting up early tomorrow, did you finish your homework? You shouldn't forget to do your homework, now." But since she had realized that this whole drawing thing had a meaning, she had had a hard time stopping. In fact, she could no longer stop herself. Then La MADRE would rush into her room: "It's one o'clock in the morning, that's enough for today, you're keeping your sister awake," then La MADRE would turn off the light for her, like when she was little. But sometimes Griselda would get up in the middle of the night to go back to the outline of a blade of grass, or to finish an ear, a hoof, an open mouth. She drew and drew, tirelessly. She spent whole nights drawing on notebooks, on those big pads that they'd bought for her when everyone was happy, but now everyone seemed to regret it.

"Calm down, rest, Griselda, you're restless, you're awfully restless."

Griselda would have liked to have gone to school at Bellas Artes.

La MADRE couldn't even stand the thought of it: Bellas Artes, Simone de Beauvoir, it all went together. "But I instilled a sense of family in you, what the hell are you going to do there?" Griselda insisted. At Bellas Artes, she could blossom, she would feel good there. But for La MADRE, only whores went to Bellas Artes, they didn't teach about charcoal drawing there, or watercolors, no, but about cocks, that's what she thought. But she didn't say it, she wouldn't have been able to say it. "Little bitch and whore" was the most she could say. "Cock" was too much for her. Someone would have had to say it for her, just to piss her off or to relieve her a little, deep down, *pija, pija, pija*. La MADRE didn't know how to say it, she had to make do with screaming: "*Basta*, enough, enough, go to bed now!"

Then her drawing pads began to disappear. La MADRE, no doubt, so that she could relax and sleep again. "Give it a break with that, will you!" But La MADRE understood nothing about it at all. As if all it took was to hide her notebooks and drawing pads, to take away her gouaches for her to stop drawing.

Since her notebooks disappeared, Griselda pounced on the boxes that were delivered to her father for the pharmacy.

She made profiles, puppets, heads from the empty Bayer boxes. She still sees the logo. Sometimes it looked like a cross, sometimes a target, with the Y right in the middle. So, she cut it out, she put eyes in it, she added horns to it, to Bayer. Well done, here, take that, Bayer. She had been doing this with her pencils and pens from high school since the gouaches had been taken away from her. But she could have done it with tomato sauce, La MADRE just did not understand. She could have done it with mud. This need. The rage she had; it couldn't be stopped just like that.

And then Griselda wanted to die

There were several, in fact, many days when she wanted to die. To die for real, you know.

The father's pharmacy was there, it was so easy, you could access the storeroom through a small door at the back of the laundry room.

First there was the day she took a box of barbiturates. She was seventeen. She swallowed the contents, guzzled the whole box! Then she lay on her back waiting for death. She then sees herself throwing up in the kitchen, or was it the bathroom? Griselda vomited while her mother shouted, she emptied her guts over the screams of La MADRE. After that, there is a blank in her memory. Maybe she just passed out. Or maybe it was more than that, maybe she had checked out completely for a moment, she had done everything to make that happen, a whole box for goodness' sake, maybe she had managed to turn the lights off. She didn't really want to die, only to die a little, just something more than some bitch with the vapors, you know, because you'd have to be a real asshole to want to die and end up just fainting. In any case, it was not enough: she sees herself still in her bed, La MADRE by her side, holding her hand, and her father standing behind. "Griselda, you gave us a real fright!" She was still there, as before, in her room, in her little bed, in their little apartment. And across the room, her little sister watched her, sitting in her ever so well-made bed, her immaculate little bed: back to square one.

A girlfriend had told her that sometimes you come out alive when you take just the same active ingredient, that an entire box or even two may not be enough to finish you off if all the tablets are identical. "That's what saved you by chance, Griselda, as you didn't know." Since her friend had told her that, Griselda had promised herself not to make the same mistake the next time she wanted to die. That next time that came quickly. Two boxes with different active ingredients, that's what she needed. With the drug storeroom at the back of the laundry room, nothing could be simpler, in theory. If it weren't for the fact that since her first attempt, the storeroom door was always double locked. Her father kept the key on him, but she had a good idea where her parents had a duplicate. How could she go and look for it, since her every movement was constantly being watched? Even her two brothers and the princess were in on it. It was impossible to go to the laundry room without her parents asking her if she needed anything. And if her parents hadn't seen her, there was always one of her brothers or the little marvel to snitch on her. And why, huh? What was it to them that she wanted to die? If they would only leave her alone, she could end it, finally escape from her shitty life that had lasted too long. But why the fuck did they give a shit, why stop her? Even her parents, what was it to them? They had a real nerve, her parents. Always saying: "Where are you going, Griselda? You need something? Just say, darling?" But damn, hell, they'd been spreading their shit around for years, they had even gone to peddle their pills in the depths of the pampas. They didn't mind poisoning half the town with Veronal or Valium, all with a smile, please and thank you: "Anything else, madam?" Even the little old lady from Calle 50, the one who staggered as she pushed open the shop door, the granny with white hair and dark glasses who had more and more trouble getting her purse out of her handbag the more she guzzled Valiums: "Two boxes of ten milligrammes, right?" It didn't bother them to sell her their crap even if the poor old woman was obviously addicted, even if with all the pills she was taking she died a little more each time she pushed the door of the pharmacy. And that's what they then used to pay for their steaks, thanks to this poison that they sold while all the time nodding their heads in approval: "There you go, madam, have a nice day!" And they had the nerve to refuse it to her when she needed it so badly.

But one day she succeeded. They couldn't always keep an eye on her. The duplicate that gave access to the stockroom was exactly where she thought it would be. "When you want to die, you have these intuitions," that's what she had said to herself as she slipped her hand into the green jar on top of the kitchen shelf, in the middle of the night, and felt straight away the metal of the key on her fingertips. "It's crazy, I suddenly know everything, understand everything, nothing can be hidden from me, I could have set up a fortune-telling firm, made it rich as a clairvoyant, but I'm going to die tonight."

While everyone is sleeping, in almost perfect silence, Griselda sneaks into the stock room and takes two boxes of different barbiturates, since now she knows: with two kinds of barbiturates, you can't go wrong.

This second time, Griselda thinks of everything. Of the creaking faucet in the kitchen, the noise of which in the middle of the night could wake La MADRE, the father or one of the three snitches. She has even thought about the tap! The day before, she hid a bottle of water on her shelf, behind the books. Despite the darkness, she finds it easily. Sitting on her bed, calmly, trying to make as little noise as possible, so as not to wake her little sister, she swallows the contents of the two boxes. With the different active ingredients. Every last pill. Then she goes to bed, calmly, oddly peaceful since death will come soon. In the house, the others sleep as if nothing was happening. This second time, she succeeded.

When, two days later, she woke up in the hospital with a tube in her arm, she didn't immediately understand where she was or what her condition was. Was she really alive? "You scared us so much, Griselda!"

It took her several more days to figure out what had happened that night.

Griselda had swallowed all the pills, many of them and of two kinds, as she had planned; no one had heard her; she had gone to bed and was already dying peacefully when her little sister started screaming in the middle of the night.

Even though everything had gone perfectly and Griselda had been able to find the key to the stock room that her father had tried to hide — for that night, nothing could stop her — and she had managed to slip into the room noiselessly, and taken two boxes of different barbiturates that she had snaffled straight away under her nightshirt in case she bumped into anyone — but no, phew, everyone was sleeping. Even though she had then carefully swallowed several dozen pills without turning on the kitchen tap — because she had thought of everything, nothing was going to prevent her from dying this time — it just had to be that night that the porcelain doll — who was nevertheless sleeping soundly when Griselda had gone back to bed, sure that this was to be her last night — had to wake up. "Mama, I'm sick! Mama, I'm sick!" cried the little one, holding her right ear. Her little sister had an ear infection. The little princess who normally was never sick, because in addition to being so beautiful and so wise, she always slept like an angel. Except for that night: "Mama, it's sore, Mama!" La MADRE had then run up, turned on the light and come across this scene: at the back of the room, little blondie was screaming, sitting up in her bed, and on the floor there were two eyes under or rather over jet-black hair. Because the head that La MADRE saw was thrown back, but as the rest of the body had not left the mattress, she had first seen black hair next to several empty tablet sachets, then two eyes, a nose and a mouth from which dripped a thin trickle of drool. It was probably because this head seemed to be mounted upside down that La MADRE had taken a while to recognize Griselda. Then she had screamed, and the father had stormed into the room before driving Griselda to the hospital where they had pumped her stomach.

Not only was she not dead, but it was the porcelain doll that had saved her.

The third time she wanted to die was a few years after all that. She was twenty-five.

For her latest suicide, Griselda opts for drastic means. It is out of the question that she fails. Barbiturates are over with. She buys a gun. It's much easier than accessing the drug stocks at the back of the laundry room. Nothing is easier in La Plata than finding a piece. Whether it be nationalist, Peronist, Marxist-Leninist or Maoist, everyone is up for a revolution and everyone can get hold of a gun for that. Without asking her any questions about her plans, a girlfriend gives her a contact in Berisso. "They will see you right." Everything is so simple, this time. Griselda has been working, so she has her own money. Since her parents agreed to let her live in her own place, even helping her to become a homeowner, convinced by her psychiatrist that things would be better this way, that it would be much better for Griselda's stability, no one has been keeping an eye on her. So, she takes the bus, goes to Berisso, and buys with her money a brand new revolver before leaving again with the weapon in her little handbag. Everything is so simple this time: "It's an automatic, super light as well, as easy to handle as a toy gun." She goes back to her place, puts the gun down on the living room table. Everything is good this time. This night will be her last. She's sure of it. And relieved, too. She picks up the gun, loads it as she has been shown, holds it to her temple, then Griselda fires a bullet into her head.

Everything went to plan. The bullet perforated her skull. This time, Griselda had succeeded. Pow! She fired the bullet inside herself. The bullet is still inside her head. Under her so-short hair, under this bare temple. It lodged itself in a recess of her brain, in a place where her head could accommodate it without damage. Without even bleeding inside.

There are places in the skull where it can take a bullet with little or no effect. These things happen, sometimes. But it is so strange and hard to think about that a head should swallow up a bullet without flinching. This kind of mystery, this sort of miracle, baffles doctors and keeps them at a distance. "We're not going to operate, no. Since the bullet slid in there and everything is fine, we are not going to do anything."

Thus, the bullet will stay inside her, until the end. So that she doesn't forget, who knows. So that she doesn't forget that she wanted to die. But to die for real, right?

She later said in court: "Many times I wanted to die. To the point that I shot a bullet into my head. But even that didn't work." The medical report confirmed: "Here it is, look." In the articles they wrote after the trial, journalists took up Griselda's strange adventure: her suicide attempts were no joke, a bullet in the head was really not a joke.

And if the bullet is still there, it's so that she doesn't forget — who could say — that it was written in the stars that she wouldn't succeed.

Everything happens very quickly

It was shortly after this episode that Griselda and Claudio met. The bullet was already stuck in her head when they began their soundless dance in the bookstore, near the Plaza Italia, and when they started seeing each other in secret, in the apartment her pharmacist father had helped her buy.

Griselda was much smaller than Claudio and ten years younger, too. She forgot herself in his arms like she was a broken doll. Back then, the scar was much more visible than it is now. "You have a piece of lead in there, do you? And you smile at me, and you kiss me?" That Griselda could pass through death to end up there in front of him, safe and sound, was so strange. Claudio stroked her left temple, the point where the bullet had entered Griselda's skull. "But all that is over now we're together..." Claudio would say, hugging her. This death that had wanted nothing to do with her had brought them closer together.

Griselda felt like everything made sense around Claudio, both what had been and what could not have been. Everything that had happened to her, everything that had eluded her, was because it was written that they should love each other. The cries of La MADRE. Her sandwiched childhood. Don Valerio's fingers. The flesh underwear stirring under her buttocks. The sky in Russian films. Her notebooks covered with drawings. The stock room at the back of the laundry room, in her father's pharmacy. The key to allow access that she had found by chance in a jar in the kitchen.

But no, not by chance.

Griselda had had to try to end it once again, to understand. To convince herself, afterwards, definitively: there was no coincidence involved. All that had to be. Like her sister's ear infection, that painful eardrum that had made her scream, alerting La MADRE to prevent Griselda from dying in peace. Everything that happened and everything that couldn't happen was because she and Claudio were destined to love each other. How could anyone doubt it? Their love was so written in advance that her skull had swallowed a lead bullet like a frog would have swallowed a fly. Gulp. The bullet in the head was the icing on the cake.

Fate had ended up transforming a piece of lead into a fly, into a cherry, into nothing at all. Just a trace of the death she had so longed for, so desired, stuck inside her so she wouldn't forget. So that she understands, above all, once and for all. *Get that in your head, little one, get that in your head, if you want, there you go*, this bullet seemed to be saying to her: *If you have to live, it's because Claudio has to bump into you again at the back of the Calle 6 bookstore. If you have to live, it's because it is written that he must love you like crazy, got it?*

That is all.

At the time, he was working in a university restaurant, but the most important thing for him was his activity in the university trade union. Even if for some time his union involvement had served, above all, to cover up his clandestine love affairs. Claudio used late meetings more and more often as an excuse to join Griselda at her house.

At first, they arranged to meet, but soon they no longer needed to consult each other, being together had become a habit, a necessity even, and her apartment was the place that Claudio hastened to after his day's work. As soon as the time came when he was sure to find her there, he ran, always climbing the steps that led to Griselda's apartment two by two. Her appearing in the doorway before him always seemed like a new miracle. Each time he cried out, relieved: "It's okay, I'm here." Then Griselda clung on to his big body.

Griselda's forehead was level with his pectorals, all she had to do was put her head in there to forget everything. Glued against him, Griselda closed her eyes and her breathing stopped.

"1974, 1975. It all happened very quickly." Griselda said at the table in Le Bûcheron.

I continued to write in the notebook that I had kept just for her story. It had been almost three hours since we had been seated at Le Bûcheron and Griselda spoke to me nonstop, without my needing to question her. But suddenly, the memories fused and intertwined.

"It all happened very quickly," Griselda repeated.

Griselda spoke of the repression of 1974 and 1975, the violence which had then redoubled in Argentina, the escalation between extreme left and extreme right groups.

It all happened very quickly.

Griselda was talking about love, too. She was talking about Claudio.
    Griselda talked about violence and love, at the same time.

Suddenly Griselda lifted up her eyes and looked at me; she had a specific date to give to me.

"October 8, 1974, write that date down, did you write it down?"

Griselda repeated it. From her seat, she glanced at my notebook to check that I hadn't made a mistake.

"That's it, October 8, 1974."

That day, in the premises of the union, a whole group watched over the bodies of two activists who had just been murdered. Griselda was there too, watching with Claudio and the others. In fact, there were many of them, about fifty people, all stunned by the explosion of violence. They wanted to show that they weren't backing down. So, after watching over the two trade unionists, they insisted on escorting the coffins to the cemetery. There were many of them walking, in silence. Even more numerous than in the premises of the union. Suspicious-looking cars were following them, people who obviously weren't their own, too. It was a funny mix, this procession. People were jostling. In the union office, they had hugged each other, cried and given each other courage. But once outside, everything had become confused. They no longer knew who was who. Just like what was happening in the whole country. The same confusion. At one point someone approached Claudio and whispered in his ear, close to his back for a moment: "You'll be next." By the time he turned around, the person had disappeared.

When Claudio told her about the scene the same evening, Griselda had the impression that she had also heard this voice in the thronging crowd. *Vos sos el próximo*. Yes, this threat, whispered into his ear. Everything that touched Claudio touched her too, that's why even if she was a bit further away, she had heard those words, slipping into her own ear, too, *el próximo*.

The *próximos* were discovered every day. But this time it was Claudio who was threatened with death.

And since everything was written in advance...

What awaited them now? So, what was the next step they would soon discover? That the next to die would be him? What if the two of them were next?

— 1974, 1975, it all happened very quickly.
Griselda was talking about violence. Griselda was talking about love. Griselda was talking about fear, too. At the same time.

She remembers: a few days after that, the police went to pick up Claudio from his home, where he was living with Janine and their children. But these policemen were the kind that could imprison people or make them disappear. Luckily, when the men came to his home, Claudio was at Griselda's. And nobody knew her address. Phew, Claudio was saved, safe in their love nest.

But the men who went to pick up her lover took away his wife and children. The day after their arrest, the children were collected by their grandparents. But not Janine, Claudio's wife, who remained in prison.

"It all happened very quickly," Griselda repeated.

After the threat slipped into the hollow of the ear of the man she loved, after his family was arrested and his wife imprisoned, Griselda and Claudio never left each other.

Now she was the one trying to reassure him: "It's okay, I'm here," Griselda would say.

But nothing was going well.

Claudio was safe, but he felt guilty.

He lived hidden away with his mistress — because that's what she was, she hadn't wanted to put it like that to herself before, but she was his mistress. The other woman. And now, when Griselda pressed herself against him, Claudio's eyes remained glued to the ceiling.

Claudio was thinking of his children, of the boys who must have been terrified by what had happened. He imagined the knocking on the door, the guys coming into their house in the middle of the night, the shouting: "Your husband, where is your husband?!" The drawers being emptied and tossed across the room, the notebooks being inspected, every piece of paper, looking for names, clues: "Where is your husband?" But you don't leave your mistress' address on a piece of paper in the marital home. That's what saved him. His double life, his lies, his cowardice.

And it was Janine who was languishing in prison, in his place. The mother of his children. Did they hurt her? Did they hit her? What was going to happen now? "It's okay, Claudio, I'm here," Griselda would say.

But no, nothing was okay.

"Things then happened very quickly," Griselda repeated.

Everything had already happened far too quickly.

Luckily, Janine's French family knew people. Connections at the highest level, including some de Gaulle in there.

Griselda knows fine that by 1975, de Gaulle was already dead.

But there was still some de Gaulle involvement. A phone call made in memory of the general, to the right person. Someone that Janine's family knew from London, from the maquis, or wherever. And voilà, the French embassy in Argentina intervened, and Janine was released. A few days later, Janine and the children took the first plane to Paris.

Everything was happening very quickly.

Everything was cracking, breaking and advancing at the same time.

Claudio's marriage, Argentina.

Love also moved forward. And no one could stop it any more.

The escape

Griselda decided to sell everything she could: the small apartment where she lived, that her father had helped her buy, and her car. "What madness, Griselda, what are you doing?" said La MADRE, as her daughter threw into an old case some things she had left at her parents' home.

But there was no time for discussions or explanations, since everything was going so quickly, you just had to go with it.

Thanks to the money they managed to put together, Claudio and Griselda went from La Plata to Buenos Aires then, without stopping, from there to Paso de los Libres, to get to Brazil. Claudio had fake documents. He had changed his face to resemble that on his passport, letting his mustache grow. He had to go first. Griselda's papers were real, no one was looking for her. As soon as Claudio was on the Brazilian side, she would go to find him.

The mad part was the plan to cross the border at Paso de los Libres. The irony of the name, when she thinks about it… Paso de los Libres was the perfect place to get busted. Every traveler was closely checked. Not just the papers, but also the faces. In Paso de los Libres, there were the police, but also snitches, a slew of outstretched fingers pointing in the shadows. A whole set of informants and grasses.

Claudio and Griselda threw themselves into the wolf's mouth.

But Claudio's fake papers were taken for real. The snitches didn't recognize him, unless they all looked away at the same time. Then it was Griselda's turn. Together they managed to reach Brazil without any difficulty, as if everything that should have been complicated and dangerous for them could not be easier.

If they had rushed into the wolf's mouth, one must believe the wolf had not wanted them.

But what about Griselda, then?

Griselda's money allowed them to pay for the next steps. In Brazil, they bought tickets to Paris.

Claudio traveled with false papers, Griselda with her papers in order.

When they reached France, one of the first things he did was to call his wife, Janine, who had gone to her parents' house with Sylvain and Damien, near the Place des Ternes. After weeks of anguish, they were finally together again. The children no longer seemed the same, the recent events had changed them so much. Two months had passed since the police had come to their home in La Plata, to take away their mother. But it seemed like it had been much longer. Griselda remembers that Claudio often told her that Sylvain and Damien's eyes were no longer the same. They had been afraid, yes, that's probably what had changed them so much.

Janine's parents had taken care of the issues with the documents, explaining with the right words and phrases that their daughter's husband had no choice, that he had tampered with a friend's passport to save his skin, find his wife and children, all of whom were French. For him, everything worked out as quickly as possible. His in-laws and his wife knew what to do.

But what about Griselda, then?

When she arrived in Bobigny, in a refuge for foreign nationals, the money she had kept from her past life had almost entirely vanished.

Everything happened so quickly, for her too. She became a refugee; Claudio guided her through the steps to take. It was much simpler than today, Griselda tells me. It was another time, really.

Everything happened very quickly, she no longer knows how, but there she was with a refugee card and a travel document, in his name, because she had fled Argentina with Claudio.

But were they still together? Did she live alone, in Bobigny?

Yes, she did in fact live alone. She finally realized it. And… Damn…

She had done all that to end up like an asshole, in a grim home. Had she sacrificed everything for him, risked everything for him just to leave her there?

Claudio was quietly installed with his wife and two children in a large apartment with his parents-in-law. Every single day, they ate on a white tablecloth.

Damn, she had been tricked… She had given up everything, left everything behind. She had risked being singled out at Paso de los Libres, disappearing there, in a kind of black hole, forever more. She had risked her life, yes. Like him, but for him. Not for a moment had she hesitated, as they loved each other. And now, when he got to Paris, he was leading a quiet and bourgeois life, her great love had ditched her to reunite with his wife and children. And her…

"But no, Griselda," Claudio would say, "that's not true, come on. Think properly, I am here, with you. I come to see you. You see… and I do love you…"

"And I do love you," to finish his list of justifications.

At the end of his little speech.

Next thing they were fucking, so that they no longer had to talk about their situation. In a refugee home in Bobigny.

Griselda started working as a housekeeper in a hotel.

Janine didn't want to hear about Griselda. The Argentinian nightmare was over, the family she had founded with Claudio was finally reunited, everything was fine.

In fact, Claudio didn't really know what to think of it all…

He felt guilty once more, this time about Griselda. It is true that she had sacrificed everything for him. Then there was everything she had told him. Everything he had guessed, too. She was alone, without a country, without a family, she had lost everything. She didn't speak French. She had a piece of lead in her head that often still hurt. It hurt terribly at times. And she had no one or nothing she could cling on to. And then there was his own existence as a privileged refugee, with his wife and children, near the Place des Ternes…

Janine did everything to keep Claudio close to her, so that he didn't go to Bobigny. She had found herself a job and some French classes for Claudio. Sylvain and Damien had started going to school, an almost normal life was falling into place.

But Griselda? He couldn't do this to her.

Very quickly, he began to alternate. He spent a night at the home in Bobigny, then a night in the beautiful Parisian apartment of his parents-in-law, with his wife, Sylvain and Damien.

But Griselda?

She had given up everything for him, damn it.

Yes, she had risked everything, to the point of putting her head in the wolf's mouth.

Of course, Claudio said he was going back to Janine to see his children. But she wasn't stupid, she knew at his in-laws, it was also Janine's and to some degree his home.

Things weren't the same between them as before. Claudio seemed distant, out of reach.

Sometimes he started talking about Angola, about revolution, he was chasing old dreams. But the next day, he was going back to his wife.

One morning at dawn, a bailiff turned up at the Bobigny refuge to certify an act of adultery.

Griselda will never forget the humiliation of the scene. The man feeling the mattress to make sure it was warm. Taking note of what clothes were on the rickety chair in her room in the home — bra, underwear, man's boxer shorts. In the next room, a baby started crying, no doubt awakened by the noise. The old African man in the room opposite stuck his head in the doorway. Griselda started to cry. Suddenly, it felt like the bullet was pounding in her skull. As if the piece of lead had come alive, as if the piece of lead was taunting her from within.

Griselda was ashamed. Griselda was scared. Griselda was lost.

So, a little later, she had this idea. What if she went to see what was happening in Argentina? President Isabel Perón had called for elections. People were disappearing, fingers everywhere were pointing out from the shadows. But what if this was the true end of this nightmare soon, the end for real?

She had nothing left of the money she had raised almost a year earlier through the sale of her apartment and her car. But she had saved part of what she had earned in Paris, doing cleaning work. She had enough to buy a ticket to Argentina. Once she was there, she would see more clearly. Claudio could divorce and then join her once the political situation had calmed down. She believed it.

Besides, she still had her Argentinian passport, which was not even fake.

No one was looking for her, so she could enter the Argentinian territory without problem. The one on the run was Claudio. What did she have to fear?

To get to Argentina, Griselda had the idea of doing it in stages. Paris-Bogota, Bogota-Caracas, Caracas-Santiago de Chile. From there, she would get to Buenos Aires. From Pinochet's Chile.

She nevertheless took her political refugee travel document in her luggage, just in case. In fact, she had two passports: the Argentinian passport, legal, normal, that of a traveling Argentinian, the only one that could allow her to return to the country. And the other, the OFPRA refugee travel document, which was just as legitimate. But which confirmed that she was not safe in Argentina, that she had requested political asylum in France.

Was this a good idea?

No.

Her refugee face

It was the beginning of 1976. Hard to imagine a worse time for her return.

Griselda will never forget the scene. She was at Santiago Airport in Chile, queuing in front of the immigration controls, her Argentinian passport in her hand, the one from before Bobigny, the one that was to allow her to return to Argentina as if nothing had happened.

But the queue wasn't moving forward.

Suddenly, the police arrived to lend a hand to the man at the desk. Then soldiers appeared — three or four heavily armed men. In a few moments, Griselda had before her a little army in blue and khaki.

A policeman began questioning the woman who was first in line. Then one of the soldiers asked her for her bag, before emptying it onto a Formica table. Meanwhile, another fingered the lining, inspecting even the leather straps that he slid from one end to the other between his fingers, to make sure that nothing had been hidden inside.

Griselda had her travel document in her bag, the paper that said that she was not only Argentinian with no issues related to the passport she held in her hand, but also that she was a refugee in France. The two were true. Suddenly, she realized her error. If the police came across her two identity documents, that would be the end.

So, Griselda took a few steps, on the spot, very conspicuously, as if she was mimicking a sudden pressing need, then she headed for the toilet.

As soon as she closed the latch, she opened her bag. The travel document was there, in a pocket. She had to destroy it, right now, she had to get rid of this thing.

Within seconds, the inside pages of her travel document had ended up in confetti at the bottom of the bowl. Phew, that was one thing sorted.

But the photo resisted her, the damn, solid thing, with her photo and the OFPRA stamp over her mug. She had one tough refugee face. Ah, if she had had scissors, a knife, a metal file, but for all she raked around in her bag, she had nothing like that. She tried to rip her face off with her fingernails. In vain. Griselda slipped her picture between her teeth. Incisors, canines, nothing helped. She barely managed to inflict a few scratches on her foreigner's face. In addition, there was the paperback cover of the document. The inside, she had shattered in seconds, but the cover was as tough as the photo. So, Griselda threw everything in the bowl and then flushed the toilet.

Griselda saw her refugee face spin like a crazed carousel right in the middle of the swirling water. Once, twice, three times she flushed that damn toilet. But as soon as the whirlpool stopped, her head was still there, resting above the cardboard cover that the water was slightly warping. That's all she managed to achieve — a blister.

The cover and the photo were too much at once, she couldn't do the two together. So, Griselda plunged her hands into the toilet, retrieved the cardboard cover — she had better try to get rid of her face first, that was the most urgent thing.

She waited once again for the cistern to finish filling up before flushing the full amount of water onto her image and sending it on its way. Then someone knocked on the door. Griselda shouted: *¡ocupado!* How long could it have been since she had been in that toilet cubicle? Griselda wanted to vomit. On the third attempt, by chance, her refugee face disappeared down the U-bend, washed away by the water.

For a moment, as she watched the photograph swirl out of sight, Griselda thought she was saved.

But he still had the hardcovers, and outside the people were getting impatient: *¿Se siente bien, algún problema?*

She felt herself perspiring, an icy sweat covered her body, like a wave descending from head to toe and back up again.

Griselda thought she was staggering, perhaps she fainted for a few moments. It is possible that the renewed knocks on the door brought her back to what she was living, or it could have been the worried voice on the other side: *¿Necesita ayuda, quiere que llame a alguien?* Griselda heard herself stammering: *No, no, todo bien*, but what to do with the hardcover, she feared that the zealous voice would end up looking for someone to take her out by force from those cubicles, so Griselda folded the cardboard cover of her travel permit one way and then the other, she transformed it into an irregular cube, a kind of dented accordion which she slipped, the best she could, between the cistern and the toilet wall. Then Griselda flushed the toilet one last time to make sure that her refugee face had gone down the drain for good, that there was no risk of it reappearing at the bottom of the bowl. It was good, it seemed to be well and truly gone. So, Griselda came out of the cubicle.

It was soon her turn for the passport check and the search.

A woman passed by her, carrying a bucket and a mop. The woman gave her a smile. Maybe even a wink. She remembers one woman for sure, but maybe there were two. In any case, she understood that they had found what had remained of her travel document behind the toilet cistern. That they had understood. Maybe her face had even reappeared at the bottom of the bowl. But if the woman smiled at her, if she winked at her, it was just to let her know she had nothing to fear, that she and her friend had taken care of everything. That they had taken it upon themselves to make the remnants of her other passport disappear.

Then, when her turn came, when the policeman started asking her questions, while a soldier emptied the contents of her bag on the Formica table, Griselda was convinced that nothing could happen to her. She remembers that despite the panicky episode in the bathroom, suddenly she could not have been calmer. No doubt that is what protected her from a thorough interrogation.

It is important to be calm.

Back to La Plata

When her sister saw her waltzing into her home in La Plata, she let out a cry. Griselda hadn't warned anyone: "What are you doing here?" Her blonde sister turned woman was whispering and screaming at the same time — it sounded like she was whispering, but she was screaming: "You're crazy, what took you to come back ?" Her sister was expecting a couple of friends for dinner, people Griselda knew. Seeing her as soon as they arrived, they started crying: "Griselda, what are you thinking of?!" The woman hid her face in her hands and the man said: "But you're going to get yourself killed, Griselda, do you know what's going on here?! Do you know what's happening right now?!" He also whispered and screamed at the same time.

The next day, Griselda went to see her father. La MADRE was no longer there. The news of her death had reached her, but it was there in the silent house that she really understood it. Her father was so happy to see her. Less surprised and worried than her sister, he took her in his arms: *Griseldita, mi amor*. Her father always loved her. But she couldn't stay there, she couldn't go back to square one under the same roof where she and La MADRE had shouted so much. Then Griselda went back to see her sister, who bored her rigid with her advice: "Don't go out until dark, Griselda, don't talk to anyone, be careful."

Griselda remembers that she had been at her sister's house for maybe four or five days without stepping outside. Then she wanted to see the Plaza Italia again, to go to the bookstore where she had met Claudio. So, Griselda tied up her hair, which at the time was shoulder length, and went out.

A man was standing by the elevator; he came up behind her. A neighbor, perhaps, but to tell the truth, she didn't really know. "You're the sister, aren't you?" Griselda just gave him a nod of her head. Once they reached the ground floor, she passed in front of the guy, then she sped off without looking back.

At the Plaza Italia, Griselda sat down on a bench, a little out of the way.

But she wasn't alone for long.

A man came to sit next to her. Was it the same one as in the elevator, her sister's neighbor who perhaps had followed her?

She doesn't really know. In the elevator, she did not get a clear view of the man who had spoken to her. This one was wearing a hat, as far as she remembers, the other was not. And this second one was familiar with her: "I know who you are, Griselda. You come from France, *yo sé quién sos.*"

Griselda said nothing.

Then the man asked her about Claudio, and she nearly choked. No doubt, he knew who she was.

This all happened on 23 March, 1976.

She is certain of the date. For this simple reason: the next day, on the radio, the coup d'état was announced.

A few days later, she took off again for Paris.

Back to Bobigny. The ultimatum

So, Griselda found a room in the same refuge for foreigners as before. And almost at the same time, a job as a cleaner in a hotel. She heard nothing from Claudio. Once, she thought he might have been in Angola, that he was following his dreams that perhaps she shared, too: she was no longer sure. Whatever he was up to, as soon as he could, he would signal to her to come and join him. But sometime after her return, Argentines who knew them both and who lived in the same refuge informed her, with a sorry look, that Claudio was not leading a revolution in Angola. Or anymore. In any case, he was back at his in-laws' apartment near the Place des Ternes with Janine and the children. Family life had lured him back. He was taking French lessons. As soon as he got a little better with the language, Janine's family would probably help him find work.

Anger overwhelmed Griselda.

She felt sullied.

And more alone than ever.

Because she had risked everything for this man. Sold everything she had; all her money had been swallowed up in their escape.

She had been humiliated. She had first understood that she was the other woman, and now she understood that she was no longer anything. And she knew now that she could no longer go back to Argentina.

So, in her bed, Griselda cried; she wept as she had before.

Griselda was not well at all.

The bullet inside her skull was beating again. It was taunting her again.

Griselda had wanted so badly to die. And now she wanted it so badly once again. As she always had done, or maybe more than ever.

She saw no other way out. At night, in her bed, when she had stopped crying, she imagined how she could do it.

When she thought about the bullet stuck in her head, Griselda cried and laughed at the same time. Tough as old boots, Griselda, how do we end this for good? It's true, damn it, *yo sé quién sos*, you don't die like that. Tough, yes, that's true. The bullet was still taunting her, she knew it well, but this time she would get there, she wouldn't let herself get away this time. Griselda wouldn't let Griselda slip through her fingers.

Did their mutual friends alert Claudio?

One day, out of the blue, he knocked on the door to her room, just after his day's work, as he used to do in La Plata: "Everything is fine, I'm here."

His own particular smell had not changed. Claudio was still just as tall. Griselda's forehead was still level with his pectorals.

As on the first day, she just had to stick her head in there to forget everything. Nothing had changed: pressed against him, Griselda closed her eyes and her breathing stopped. In her head, suddenly, there was peace.

Then everything started again, as it had been before her trip to Argentina.

At best, she had the man of her life two out of three nights. At worst, once a week.

But one evening, Griselda did not run to open the door for him before pressing her forehead against his chest. One evening, Griselda was late to open, then she looked up at Claudio to give him an ultimatum.

"Because sometimes that is what you have to do with men," that is exactly what Griselda said to me.

Then she glanced at my notebook, she wanted to make sure that I had in fact noted that, one evening, she said to Claudio: "I have had enough, no more. It's simple, either you stay with Janine, or you stay with me. If it is with Janine, I don't want to see you ever again."

Claudio chose Griselda. And everything that came with her: the downbeat neighborhood, the lack of money. Divorce. Instead of the Place des Ternes, a refuge in Bobigny. Proof that he loved her.

He chose whatever came next, too. But he didn't know about that. But who could have known about any of that?

"You know about what came next"

"You know about what came next," Griselda told me.

She became pregnant for the first time.

Then Father Adur found them jobs as caretakers at T. High School.

When they moved there, Griselda's belly was already huge.

The priest married them in the little chapel at the back of the courtyard.

"But I already told you that," Griselda said.

Flavia was beautiful. Calm and smiling from day one. As soon as she was born.

"Did you see how beautiful she is?"

Flavia was the child she dreamed of, the child she would have liked to have been, too.

Flavia had fine features, large dark eyes like hers but much more beautiful. She had simply taken the best from her father and mother. She was always the perfect child. And she was her daughter, her own! And how hard she works, and how brave she is. How free she is.

"Have you seen her photos?"

I nodded. Flavia is an excellent photographer, she publishes regularly in the press, her work is respected. Griselda is proud of her daughter. She suddenly lowers her eyes and blushes as she smiles, so proud to be the mother of that girl. So proud of her courage. Flavia is slight, petite, with a slender look. But she is anything but fragile. Flavia is incredibly strong. She often goes on assignments in the most difficult situations. Illness, war and poverty do not stop her. Her reporting has taken her to Colombia, Ethiopia, Congo, Guinea, refugee camps in northern Iraq — at times of epidemics, tensions, and conflicts. She is not afraid to put herself in physical danger. The question does not even seem to occur to her. It doesn't stop her, anyway. Flavia wants to bring back images from places where people suffer, struggle and fight. She *must* bring back images, so that we know, so that we see. It's her job and that's what matters to her. Griselda can be proud, yes.

Enough to erase all the humiliations, all the wickedness of La MADRE.
She was not blonde, like the princess of La MADRE's dreams. But Flavia was much more than a princess, no doubt about it, and she had come out of her own womb.
"And you see what she's become!"

It was Father Adur who baptized Flavia, in the chapel where he had married them. As soon as they moved to T. High School, everything happened there. Between the lodge, the small, enclosed garden at the end of the courtyard, the garbage cans to take out…

Father Adur lived for a time in the high school, in a small room on the other side of the courtyard. Other priests lived there too, perhaps a dozen or so at most.

Griselda remembers that at the end of the day, when the school had already closed its doors for everyone else and the courtyard was silent again, they would hear Father Adur who, from the other side of the courtyard, would call to them: *Vecinos, vecinitos,* in a cheerful voice. It sounded like he was singing, maybe it was the chorus of an old song, a song she didn't know; anyway he always called out to them like that: *Vecinos, vecinitos,* following the same melody. When Griselda or Claudio came out of the lodge and waved to him, Father Adur would come down to drink a few mates with them. If the weather was nice, they would be in the garden, their little square in miniature. This went on until the day he left T. High School to return to Argentina before disappearing in Paso de los Libres. Yes, in Paso de los Libres, that's where their benefactor disappeared forever. In 1980, at the same place where, a few years earlier, Claudio and Griselda had been saved.

Claudio, Griselda, and Flavia lived in one room.

Then there were the two boys. That made five of them in their little lodge. So, Claudio had the idea of building two mezzanines.

"…but you must remember that," Griselda said to me.

I should remember that. Griselda is right.

That's because I knew Griselda and Claudio a long time ago. I also went to T. High School several times, when Claudio and Griselda housed my father. That lasted several months. It was shortly after his release, after he had spent six years in prison in Argentina, the Argentina he had just left even though he was on parole. Because people were still disappearing there, and he was afraid. But my parents had decided to separate, so my father had gone to live with Claudio and Griselda while waiting to come up with a solution.

After that dark period that I wrote about in three books: *Manèges, Le bleu des abeilles*, and *La danse de l'araignée*, my father lived there for a while. In this same small lodge already occupied by five people. Claudio and Griselda's last child, Boris, had just been born.

"Your father was his godfather, you know?"

No, I didn't know.

Or I must have known, but I forgot.

Claudio and my father had met years earlier in Cuba, where they had become friends. They had hung out together in La

Plata, before my father was imprisoned. Then they reunited in this Parisian exile. There, they had helped each other as best they could.

I was fourteen when I met Claudio, Griselda and their three children in Paris. I really should remember that — far more distant times are etched in my memory with incredible clarity. But my memories of Griselda, Claudio and their three children at T. High School are very hazy. The images overlap. I see a child in a highchair, but I cannot tell if the child whose image has stuck with me is Boris or Sacha. Their features merge with those of Flavia, too.

Griselda sees that my memory is floundering.

"One day you came to eat an asado. You were coming back from vacation; it was the end of summer. After lunch, you stayed for quite a while. You must remember that, I'm sure."

Griselda describes their lodge to me. The two mezzanines, one for them, another for the children. When they put my dad up, he was sleeping on the couch, just below. Sometimes there were six of them in this tiny space. But they did not hesitate to take him in. They loved my father very much; they were happy to help him. Then my father left.

"You don't see how it was? Don't you remember?" asks Griselda.

From their mezzanine, the parents' one, Griselda could see Flavia, Boris and Sacha in their beds.

In fact, the mezzanines looked like two huge rafts. And all she had to do was turn her head towards the children to understand that it was the children's mezzanine that was in front. The parents' mezzanine always remained behind, bringing up the rear, so that the parents could keep an eye on them. Her, especially. She didn't want to lose sight of them. How reassuring that their two mezzanines were exactly on the same level. You see, as Griselda says, she has always been a mother hen. Yes, she has always brooded over them.

Griselda smiles. Griselda becomes serious. She seems far away, a long way away. Griselda is silent.

Then she starts talking again.
Between 1978 and 1984, she was never more happy.
"Happy, truly."

She looks me in the eyes. She wonders if I understand what she's telling me. That what she tells me is true. Maybe she wants to make sure I write it down in my notebook.

She was happy, she had never been so happy.

I write it down.

With her three children close to her. Happy, yes.
The children, on their mezzanine, were just opposite or in front, it all depends on how you look at it. Almost within reach.

Griselda's eyes are bright and moist at the same time.

With these two mezzanines that Claudio had installed in the lodge, it was as if they had created another floor. Except it wasn't a real floor. Or even, a floor with gaps in it.
So, there it was: there were the children, there was the garden.

Like a square in miniature, really, and just for them.

Claudio had planted roses there; she took care of the vegetable garden. They were happy. She was happy. Very.

It was small, but they had done their best to fit everything in there, in their lodge.

Until that incomprehensible Friday.

"You know what happened next, don't you? That day, you know?" asks Griselda.

I nod yes.

That day

One cannot say that Griselda *remembers* what happened.

When she calls upon her memory, the feeling she has is very different.

What is it, then, what name to give to this faculty that allows her to say what happened on that day?

Griselda doesn't remember, no. But she *has knowledge of* that day. She knows. So, she can say certain things.

On Mother-Tortoise Day, Griselda had a hard time getting up.

Her head. She was in so much pain.

Flavia had to manage on her own to prepare something. Like a big girl, she made a cold milk with lots of chocolate. She dressed herself, too, as Griselda had taught her. But Flavia had never gone to school without her mother, that's why she drummed on the covers, why she insisted. She didn't want to miss school, her mother had to get up.

Griselda ended up doing it.

She dressed silently, effortlessly, despite the pain. But that's not the word. The pain that for so long gnawed away at her skull had suddenly become something else — Griselda was in a condition beyond pain.

Her gestures were mechanical. She made them one after the other without pausing. Something had been set in motion: the first gesture that morning had given impetus to all the others. It was as if someone had wound up a clock that had stood still for a long time, a clock that Griselda didn't know existed, but that someone had put their hands on to wind up the mechanism that morning. The gears clicked into each other; the movement was launched.

She helped Flavia to put on her coat, slip her hands into the blue gloves that stuck out from her sleeves, connected to each other inside the coat by a long string. She also helped her put on her balaclava.

She did the same with Boris and Sacha. She dressed them in their coats, she took care to cover their ears well, to slip their hands into their mittens; mittens are always easier with the little ones. The boys were still in their pyjamas, but it didn't matter, it was only a few minutes, all she had to do was cross the street to drop Flavia off at school, just across the street. The most important thing was that they put on their big socks and their boots, under their pyjama bottoms so as not to leave any part of their calves exposed.

All four of them crossed the street.

Griselda sees herself in the middle of the road and then on the sidewalk opposite.

Yes, she sees herself, it's weird.

As if she, Griselda, the one who is telling me all this, had actually found herself above the group she was part of with the three children. As if Griselda had held a camera that day to film the scene from above, as if she had witnessed it all through a lens or a filter. As if Griselda, from waking that morning, had been a drone above herself, or at least above part of herself, if it weren't for the fact that at the time nobody knew about drones. That's why she *knows* what happened that day without actually remembering. Griselda does not remember from inside the body crossing the street, from the body taking Flavia, Boris and Sacha. She does not remember from inside what her body was, nor from what it has become. She does not remember from inside the body saying goodbye to Flavia at the school gate, before she walked back with Boris and Sacha. But she sees all that, she *knows*.

Back in the lodge, Griselda prepares the boys' breakfast then she lies down on the sofa, under the children's mezzanine. Her body is heavy, especially her head. Like a rock or a piece of concrete.

But soon she gets up and, in front of a small standing mirror that she sets up on the large table, she begins to put on make-up.

The kids carry on playing. They do not ask to go outside, contrary to what they usually do. It's so cold, their brief outing was enough for them. Boris and Sacha run after each other around the large table, the only table, the all-purpose table. One of the two boys climbs up to the mezzanine, he comes straight back down with a bag full of toy cars. They play races on the table, then on the chairs, the cars go up along the legs in one direction then in the other. Those little cars don't know gravity, they can even whiz under the tray, hood down, wheels up. The children call out, imitating the sound of engines at full speed. Each has two cars, one in each hand. In fact, Boris and Sacha are not playing races, one cannot say that one of their racing cars is behind or in front of another, their cars are going full speed ahead, they're just trying to get them to go as fast as possible. Boris and Sacha shriek with laughter.

Meanwhile, Griselda is doing her make-up.

Until the colors she has in front of her end up completely obscuring her face.

Then she crosses the yard, enters the building where Claudio is working. And there she calls him, from the doorway. She calls for help, but he doesn't understand. He tells her to piss off, he rejects her. "Just beat it, will you!" She withdraws.

Her footsteps lead her back into the lodge.

She goes to the bathroom.

She runs water, filling the bathtub to the brim.

She undresses Sacha and plunges him into the bathtub.

The water floods out, all over the bathroom floor.
　　She has put far too much water in, so the child's body makes the bath overflow.

The water soaked her knees resting on the tiles, then went up along her thighs, as if she were sharing Sacha's bath a little.

She needs to take care of him. She must protect him. She needs to get her child to safety.

Under her eyes, there, below, the mechanism triggered when she woke up that morning escapes from her.

Griselda is above the bathtub; it is from on high that she sees the scene. On high that she is terrified, mute, but she would like to scream.

Down below, the woman she sees is convinced.
　　She must wash Sacha, protect him. So, she presses his head. The child lets her do it. A hand on his head is enough.

When Sacha stops moving, she pulls him out of the water, takes him in her arms, then wraps him in his white bathrobe which she quickly ties around his waist.

Her chest now is also soaked. Her own chest.

It looks like she's coming out of the sea, that they both just got out of the water. Like two castaways, except that one of them is no longer breathing.

She lays the child on the sofa.

But she realizes that she has not put his bathrobe on properly. So, she undoes and reties the knot of the belt around Sacha's waist.

Two identical loops, perfectly symmetrical, sit on the belly of the child. He is safe.

On the other side of the room, Boris watches them. That's probably why he's screaming.

He doesn't want to take a bath. That's probably why he is thrashing about.

That is why, even though he's smaller than Sacha, she has such a hard time keeping his head under the water. That she needs to press with all her might, that this time she needs both hands.

When Boris stops moving, she is soaked from head to toe. When she in turn puts him in his bathrobe, a puddle forms at his feet.

The water has come right up to them, the water accompanies them.

On the sofa, she places the child next to his brother.

For him, too, she undoes and then reties the knot of the belt that holds the white bathrobe at waist level. The two loops on the child's belly are now identical to those on his brother's belly.

Although the children are not the same age, there on the sofa they look like twins.

Like La MADRE, you would think that Griselda had twins. That they are there, side by side.

That she is above them, but a little beside them too, near the sofa. As she is also partly there lying down. In Boris' body. Or in Sacha's.

Then all those bits of herself come together, up above. She wants to yell, to scream. But this cry does not exist, it cannot exist, this cry is impossible.

It is THE CRY. The one that has always escaped her and this time escapes her forever more.

Her image, down below, leaves the lodge.

She finds herself in the courtyard and almost immediately in the street, on the other side of the road.

This time, she is the one pounding on the door of Flavia's school.

As soon as the school guard opens the door for her, she says, "My daughter has to come with me, I've come to pick her up."

She needed to see Flavia, right away.

The guard hesitates.

For the woman in front of her is soaked. On her face, her makeup has run.

Despite the cold, she has no coat. She looks like she fell into a pool only to jump right out there where she stood. The face garishly made up and washed away, on the threshold of winter. But she is the mother of a prepatory class student, so the guard lets her go upstairs. In the corridors, there is no one, all the children are in class.

Griselda sees her daughter on the other side of the glass, but Flavia does not see her.
   Only the Mistress sees her shipwreck face.
   The Mistress comes out into the hallway.
   "I must take Flavia," Griselda says. "She has to come with me."
   But the Mistress says: "No, that is not possible."
   She insists.
   "No," says the Mistress, "school is not over."
   She moans. She begs.
   But the Mistress says: "No." Again and again, she says: "No."
   So, head down, she leaves.

She left a puddle of colored water in front of the classroom. From above, as Griselda sees it, it looks like a pond, a lake, a blurry sea.
   She turns back. Leaves the door open behind her.
   The historic cold snap is irrelevant.
   The woman that Griselda sees from above does not fear the cold. She no longer feels anything. Or she feels things differently, in an incomprehensible way. Indecipherable.
   She does not even feel that some of her hair is now covered in frost.

The scene ends there.

At the foot of the children, lying wrapped in their bathrobes.

The sequel — she not only does not remember it; she also does not see it. The camera above her went blank.

Griselda did not wake up for a long time. A long time after that day.

2

A generation can learn a lot from another, but what is human in the literal sense, it cannot learn from the one that preceded it. In this regard, each generation begins as if it were the first, it does not have a different task from the one that preceded it, nor does it exceed it [...]. Thus, no generation can begin other than at the beginning, not one younger generation has a lesser task than the previous generation.

SØREN KIERKEGAARD,
Fear and Trembling

And I walk alone, in the night, equidistant from heaven and earth.

JEAN-LUC LAGARCE,
It's Only the End of the World

FLAVIA

What the stories hide

We were at Le Bûcheron.
Flavia had just given me the images that had remained with her from Friday, December 14, 1984, those that marked the beginning of my investigation.
I had jotted them down, trying to keep the outlines as precise as possible: in my notebook there were four individual blocks preceded by a dash, four fragments that I had carefully collected. Like those buried relics that are unearthed, those pieces of broken pottery that archaeologists brush gently before numbering them.

Four images, four fragments of that day.

ONE is the mother tortoise who does not wake up, even if Flavia drums on the bedcovers, calls her and insists.
TWO is the face of her father at school on the other side of the glass, his head without eyes, without a mouth, without a nose.
THREE is the mathematics exercises that the Mistress sets for Flavia while the other children are gone, those other problems that never end.
FOUR is the lady in uniform in the police car and Flavia's fear of being talked about on TV: "Oh no, so long as we don't appear on TV."

I finished jotting her fourth memory in my notebook, then Flavia fell silent for a long while. I put my pen down for a moment and looked at her.

A few weeks earlier, Flavia had turned forty.

And Flavia was right. That age was damn weird.

On that first meeting, when she had barely sat down, it was one of the first things she said to me: "I've just turned forty!" Because she really couldn't believe it. Because forty years like fifty is always unreal to the person who lies hidden underneath.

But not only that.

By sitting down in front of me at Le Bûcheron Flavia had no doubt become aware of the wait. Of the time that had passed without anything truly happening. Of the time that had only glided over the little girl that she was.

I understood this when I looked at her, after having noted down the fourth image that she still had from that day.

She was forty years old yet, in front of me, her eyes were six. We were at Le Bûcheron on November 1, 2018, but Flavia had been talking to me from December 14, 1984. And after passing to me what she had kept from that day, she fell silent. As if her silence were an echo of that day.

Then she resumed her story.

Flavia spoke then of Griselda's incarceration.

In theory, it was much later that she was told that her mother, at the time, was no longer living with them because she had gone to prison. She can't say exactly when she found that out. But in reality, she had understood it long before anyone told her.

It's weird: the lies people tell children.

Often, children pretend to believe the stories they are told to reassure the adults. To give themselves a little peace and quiet, too. It is that, if children show adults that they are not fooled by their spiel, grown-ups hasten to patch up their lies and plug the cracks, finally to create even bigger fibs. This prospect discourages children in advance. Because if the adults overdo it, if they push things a little too far, the children feel obliged to protest (you shouldn't take them for idiots anyway) and the matter becomes even more painful. It is usually to spare themselves all of this that children pretend to believe the lies of adults. This story of the big house where her mother was resting up, Flavia knew very well that it was not true. But when her father would say to her: "We'll go to see your mother where she's resting," she would reply: "Yes, let's go and see Mama there."

She had also understood many things about her brothers.
There had been the morning of that day and, after that, Flavia had never seen Boris or Sacha again.
To explain their disappearance, she had been told of a terrible accident with water and electricity, a misfortune which had sent her little brothers: "to heaven." Flavia knew that this story of heaven had to do with death but, like death, it is nowhere and she preferred to imagine Boris and Sacha on high. She imagined her little brothers on a plump, fluffy cloud, moving just above her head. She often pictured them barefoot, with wet hair, playing with light bulbs and sockets, laughing out loud. But you just can't do that, they should not have done that. Water and electricity can't go together, it's far too dangerous — that's what Flavia thought to herself when she pictured them that way.

Other times, on their cloud, her little brothers no longer laughed at all. They clutched electric wires in their hands that were actually lightning bolts that they brandished. Like the king of the gods did — her favorite — in her book on Greek mythology. Except that Boris and Sacha were neither strong nor bearded. They were very small and, wet as they were, these flashes did not bode well... "No bolts, no lightning, no!" Flavia closed her eyes. She held her eyelids closed tightly, very tightly. She tried to alert Boris and Sacha, by telepathy. To make them understand, up there.

Deep down, Flavia knew perfectly well that it was all just stories. But she also knew that what she had been told and all the stuff she was imagining was much better, for now, than saying or hearing what really happened. Much better than putting words to what had happened that day.

Even if Flavia said nothing, she had understood a lot of things. Many more things than adults imagined.

Nightmares and the heart

After that day, Flavia left the lodge at the T. High School and she never again set foot in the place where she had started preparatory class, where the letters had one day formed words for her, where she had known the person that she long called: "Mistress."

The evening of that day, after being taken away by the police, Flavia was dropped off at the home of Janine, Claudio's ex-wife. She stayed there for a fortnight, without going to school. Time passed slowly at Janine's.

Of Claudio's first two children, those he had with his first wife, only the youngest, Sylvain, still lived with his mother. He was almost twenty years old and was studying history at the Sorbonne. Flavia remembers having shared his room at that time, and also his kindness and sweetness. She liked him enormously.

She also remembers that Sylvain and Janine found her even wiser than before, so kind and quiet since that day. "Excessively wise, way too much, this child needs to talk, to say something." Flavia had overheard one of their conversations in the kitchen.

Sylvain always suggested that she should draw. Whatever came into her head, whatever was: "on her heart," he said.

But Flavia didn't understand what "on the heart" meant. Why the heart? Why on it?

Then Sylvain said: "Anything that goes through your head, even nightmares if you want, it's good to draw your nightmares, then you slip the sheets of paper into a drawer and you feel better."

But Flavia wasn't sure how to draw her nightmares.

Sometimes she felt like she could visualize them, so she started drawing. But very quickly, she stopped. Because, no, the drawings were not quite right.

Her nightmare was playing hide and seek with her, and was very good at it.

It was clever, her nightmare, very clever. When she felt like she had put her finger on it, there was always a point when it slipped away from her.

"I don't know what it looks like anymore, I can't see its face anymore," Flavia said: "I don't know what it looks like anymore, my nightmare."

Then Sylvain would read her stories. He would say to her: "Just because you've already learned to read doesn't mean you shouldn't be read stories, right?" They both sat cross-legged, then Sylvain read.

Sylvain was right: it wasn't at all like when Flavia read by herself. When Sylvain read, the story flowed without difficulty and, listening to it, she had the impression that images passed before her eyes, even when were no illustrations in the book.

Flavia clearly remembers one specific day in the apartment where Janine and Sylvain lived. One of those days when she suddenly found herself frozen in front of the sheet of paper that Sylvain had given her to draw on. If Flavia was stuck there, it was because the nightmare she had started to draw had once again hidden itself, which is why she could no longer continue her drawing.

So, Sylvain had an idea.

He took Flavia's favorite book, the one she had put on the bedside table, so she always had it next to her, her illustrated book on Greek mythology and gods. And that day, when they were both sitting on the floor, on the parquet floor, Sylvain read to Flavia the story of Medea.

Medea's story

The book says that Medea is the daughter of the king of Colchis. She's a princess, a bit of a goddess too, but above all she's a magician. That is the first thing to remember. Medea knows Nature and her secrets. She has long black curly hair, necklaces and embroidered jewelry. Medea's arms are long too: she raises them, she waves them.

But soon something happens that is even more important than magic: Medea sees Jason. In fact, this is where it all begins.

Jason landed in Colchis with his companions, the Argonauts, who came to search for the Golden Fleece. And as soon as Medea lays eyes on him: *a fierce fire ignites in her heart*, the book says.

It is from the heart of Medea that the book speaks.

The Fleece is in the hands of her father, the King. But Jason needs it at all costs, to become king in turn, at home in Iolcos, to repair the injustice he suffered in his country, where his uncle Pelias usurped the throne. Jason wants the Golden Fleece, he needs it.

Flavia turns her face to her brother.

"But what is the Fleece? What is the Golden Fleece?"

"No one knows for sure. But it is something very precious, a bit like a treasure," answers Sylvain.

What is certain is that Medea's father has no desire to part with this precious object, so he says to Jason that, to have it, he will have to accomplish three feats. He will first have to tame two huge bulls with hooves and horns of bronze, two fearsome beasts that spit fire from their nostrils. But that's not all. After having tamed them, he will have to hitch them to a plough and get these beasts to till a parched field. But that still won't be enough. To earn the Golden Fleece, he will have to perform a third feat: sow dragon teeth in the furrows that the bulls will have dug.

In the King's mind, it's a bit like asking Jason to reach for the moon or to stop the course of the day, to make it that the night never comes. *I ask him the impossible*, thinks the King. *Jason will never achieve these feats; he will die and the Fleece will remain in my hands.* The King of Colchis believes that the bulls' fire protects him.

But the King failed to see what was happening with his daughter. He didn't understand anything, the old King.

A violent fire was kindled in Medea's heart: in this story, it really is the most important thing.

This fire is much stronger than that exhaled from the nostrils of bronze monsters. Even stronger than the one spat out by the dragons and all other creatures. Medea loves, so nothing will be impossible for Jason. She will put her magician's powers at his service, she is already doing so — but on condition that he marries her and takes her away, she whispers to him secretly. Jason accepts. Because Medea is beautiful and Jason wants to take away the Fleece.

What leads him to say yes to Medea? Does he prefer the Fleece to the woman in front of him?

In Medea's eyes, that doesn't matter. She burns enough for two: that's what she tells herself.

But isn't it dangerous, the fire spitting from the bronze bulls' nostrils? Very dangerous, even?

Deep down, Medea laughs, she is already having fun with this story of impossible feats. The fire within her is so powerful. *It'll be fine, you'll see.* Medea laughs. *It's nothing, all that, Jason. The impossible thing that my father asks you to achieve is within your reach, because I am here.*

When the trials come, when Jason advances towards the bulls, when the beasts begin to spit fire, to strike the dusty ground with their bronze hoofs, threatening Jason with their terrible horns, his companions are afraid for him. But not Medea. That's because she gave Jason a salve of enchanted herbs.

When Jason gets close to the bulls, the beasts become docile and submit: first feat accomplished. Immediately, they drag the plough, splitting the land that the king believed to be forever dry and sterile: second feat achieved. Then Jason sows the dragon's teeth, which germinate immediately and give birth to vigorous bodies: that's the third feat done. But a new and terrible danger then stands before Jason. It is that the bodies born from the teeth of the dragon now form an army of men of phenomenal strength and, by a new miracle: *the warriors wield weapons born with them*, says the book. At this moment, Jason's companions are gripped by dread — the Argonauts cry. But not Medea. She prompts Jason to throw a magic stone into the middle of the formidable warriors. Then each of them believes they are to be attacked by one of their own, and they kill each other to the last. *They fall victim to a civil war*, the book says.

Nothing is impossible for Jason; will the King understand? For nothing is impossible for Medea, did the King understand that?

No, he doesn't understand. And he has no intention of keeping his promise: even if Jason has accomplished all his feats, the King refuses to give him his treasure.

So, since that is how things are, Medea puts the dragon that guards the Fleece to sleep. For nothing is impossible for Medea. She seizes it, then with Jason and his companions — for now she is fully on their side — they leave Colchis. With Medea's younger brother as hostage.

The King is furious, and he sets off in pursuit with his ships.

Then Medea kills and dismembers her brother and throws away the pieces of his body as the Argonauts' boat advances. Each time that her father and his men see a piece of the prince's body in the water, they stop to fish it out. This is how Medea, Jason and his companions manage to escape the King of Colchis.

But when they arrive in Iolcos, Jason understands that his uncle, the usurper, has no intention of giving him the throne that is rightfully his.

So, he asks Medea to avenge him.

In front Pelias's daughters, Medea cuts the throat of an old ram, slices it up and plunges the pieces of the old beast into a cauldron of boiling water and magic herbs. Immediately, a young lamb all pink and bleating emerges from the cauldron. Incredibly, Medea is able to reverse the passage of time! *Do the same with your father and he will become a vigorous young man again*, says Medea. Then the king's daughters cut their father's throat, dismember him, and throw his body into boiling water. But Pelias does not emerge from the pot as a young man. He ends up in a broth.

The man she loves is avenged. But now Medea and Jason must once again flee. They leave for another exile.

They then arrive in Corinth, where King Creon grants them asylum.

There Medea and Jason are very happy. In the story of Medea, there is suddenly a lull. They are both so happy that the book barely mentions that happiness. It's their secret. A secret of love that lasts for several years. Two boys are then born to Jason and Medea.

Everything is going well until the day Jason falls in love with the daughter of the King of Corinth. And since Jason is handsome, since he's strong — Medea knows that! — Creon would very much like him to marry his daughter and succeed him on the throne.

It's no doubt a hell of an opportunity for Jason. He who could not be king in Iolcos. A pretty princess, a throne offered to him. A life of luxury.

The problem is Medea.

Jason tries to explain to her. This new love, this opportunity: for him, the refugee. Behold, he will become king of the land that welcomed him! But Medea must go. She should understand… Go back. Go away.

Medea breaks down.

But what does he believe?

For Jason, she betrayed her father. She fled her country. Killed her brother. Dismembered the body of the young prince, which she threw into the sea.

For Jason, she concocted a king's broth. Fled again.

And he leaves her? For a princess and a throne?

But… And Medea?

And what about Medea?

Medea is mad with rage. She's mad with pain. She is lost.

The fire of yesteryear, the eternal fire, begins to burn strong, so strong.

It's a bonfire now. Can't Jason see this? Doesn't he see how she burns?

No, Jason doesn't understand. Not really, not enough… He doesn't understand her boundless pain, he doesn't understand what this pain is capable of.

But suddenly it seems like Medea is changing. Jason thinks so, he no longer sees her fire.

She wants to honor the Princess of Corinth — so that she accepts the children that Medea had by Jason, so that she does not chase them away and that they can stay with their father. So, Medea gives the beautiful princess a gift worthy of her: she sends her some fabric and a crown braided with gold.

As soon as the princess receives the presents, she is subjugated.

But how naive she is, the Princess. Naive as princesses are.

She really believes that Medea finally bowed down to her? That she accepts her fate, that she will slip away to let the new lovebirds bill and coo in peace?

But that's because she didn't understand either. She has understood nothing about the fire that burns inside Medea.

As soon as the Princess puts on her adornments, the scene takes an appalling turn. A white foam comes out of her mouth, her eyes roll back and leave their sockets. The fabric begins to bite the flesh of the Princess of Corinth. On her head, the crown bursts into flames.

That's it, the princess is on fire.

Then her father, old Creon.

Then the palace, ravaged by fire. And the whole city.

That is how powerful Medea's fire is.

The pain and the rage are such that she can no longer extinguish this fire.

It is stronger than anything. Fire wins.

So much so that Medea suddenly sees herself in the middle of the blaze.

She who had Nature in her hands, the elements, and the entire Universe at her mercy, here she is burning like a log, there before her own eyes.

And, possessed by the Fire, Medea stabs the children she had by Jason. Her own children, yes. Such is the unbearable nature of her anger and pain.

Wandering

Flavia and her father then entered a period of wandering, living here and there while finding new accommodation. This itinerant life lasted only a few weeks, but in Flavia's memory, those weeks felt as long as very long years.

There had been that day. Then it all fell apart. For a long time, everything had been falling apart.

It was Micky who first put them up in a housing project in Créteil that consisted of four huge towers around a kind of sandbox. Micky lived in a three room apartment with his children, two boys who spent their time screaming and clutching each other's necks.

Flavia remembers hating living there, spending whole nights wide-eyed, staring at the ceiling, fearing that at any moment the cracked kitchen window would fall into a thousand pieces. Or that the rickety shelf above Claudio and Flavia's heads would finally cave under Micky's junk: books with torn covers, empty beer cans, greasy yellow bits of cardboard pizza boxes. And those rancid smelling, capless lipsticks that made Flavia nauseated. On the couch that served as their bed, her father quickly fell into a deep sleep. But not Flavia: for days and days, her body and mind remained on the lookout.

Later, Claudio and Flavia went to live with a couple of friends in Les Lilas, Tonio and Carole, in a house that felt like a house this time, with blue curtains, a checkered tablecloth and napkins cut from the same fabric. At Tonio and Carole's, there was a bed for Claudio and another just for her. There, Flavia remembers having finally slept.

Until the day her father found an apartment in a tower in the north of Paris. As soon as they settled there, Flavia resumed her preparatory year at school. Except it was at another school. The school before, she couldn't go back there. Just as she could no longer return to the T. High School or to that lodge which during all these years had been their home, where she had been born, that space she had always known.

After that day, all those things had gone forever.

The coin

Flavia specifically remembers a few visits she made to her mother.

She and Claudio always waited in a room before seeing Griselda. It was a long, very long wait.

She sees herself again, sitting on a bench, moving her legs back and forth like you do on a swing when you try to go a little higher. But Flavia was swinging her legs on a bench fixed to the floor, so nothing was happening.

She remembers some strange details; she doesn't really know why.

One day, a man was with them in this same room. He was sitting on the same bench as Flavia and Claudio. Like them, the man had come to visit someone. A woman, of course. His daughter, his wife, his sister, who knows? But a woman, like her mother, since all this happened in the room where visitors to the Fleury Detention Center were waiting. Flavia knew it even though she also knew not to say anything. Not to pronounce these words, detention center, prison. Neither in front of her father nor in front of her mother, when they would all be together in the small room where they were soon to meet up. Her father wanted her to believe in the nursing home idea. There had been water, electricity, a terrible accident; her brothers were on a cloud in the sky and now her mother was resting up, in this place where they waited before they could see her. That's what her father had told her, and Flavia felt she had to show him that he had been right to do so. After the horror and dread of that day, she had to show him that he had done well to tell her all that. This story of a home where her mother needed to rest was the only idea that had come to Claudio. This story protected her, it protected them both a little, he thought. Flavia had understood this and she wanted to reassure her father. So, she played her role, she made sure she did not show any doubt. She believed in all of this, thought her father. *At least she believes it*, that's what he was probably thinking.

Flavia was swinging her legs as usual, both at the same time, back and forth. And sometimes one and the other, alternately, as if she were skating.

The other man waiting came up to them.

He told her that he had a daughter the same age as her. She glanced around, looking for the girl. "No, she's not here," the man said. "But you look a lot like her, she's pretty and always as good as gold. Just like you."

Then the man took a coin out of his coat pocket. He said: "Look."

Immediately, Flavia stopped moving her legs.

The man stuck the coin in his right hand, then closed it. He seemed proud, oddly pleased with himself. He widened his eyes as he smiled broadly, his eyebrows were like two circumflex accents above his gray eyes. Suddenly, the man drew a large circle in the air before blowing onto his clenched fist. For a brief moment, he pressed his fist against his other hand, then he called: "Voilà!" When the man unclenched his fingers, the coin was no longer there. Obviously, he was waiting for Flavia to marvel.

But his trick was useless, she had seen it all, the coin was in his left hand, the one the man was holding closed now. "But there it is, in your other hand…" Flavia said. The man pulled a face. He was as disappointed as she was. He had wanted to do some magic, but in his trick there was no magic at all.

"Not only are you good and pretty, but you're also very intelligent," the man said. "Wait a minute, I'll show you something else…"

So, the man took a piece of paper and a black pencil out of his pocket. He put the coin on the bench, then the paper on top of it, and began to scribble furiously. The man rubbed the lead against the paper, very hard and at top speed. His hand was moving so fast that at times you couldn't see it. The sheet then began to be covered with gray lines, lines that looked like a big stain.

Then suddenly, in the middle of the gray, the image of the coin appeared.

It was the coin that was sitting just below.

It looked as if it had passed through the sheet, that it had pierced it. Yet the coin was still hidden and the paper intact. This time, it really was magical, yes, much more so than the disappearance and the failed reappearance of this same coin. On the piece of paper, you could see the female sower figure that was on the back of one franc coins. The right hand, the one that sows, was in full flow. Flavia had never paid attention to it, that woman had never interested her, but this was different. You could see everything. Under her Phrygian cap, the sower's hair blew in the wind. You could even see the rays of the sun at the back of the scene. From the sheet, Flavia read aloud: "French Republic." She had never paid any attention to any of this.

On that bench, she had the impression of looking at a one franc coin for the first time. Even as the coin was still hidden: there it was, the magic of it. The coin was still covered by the scrap of paper, but Flavia could see it much better than when she had it in her own hands.

Then she smiled, happy and troubled at the same time. The man was awfully proud. He handed her the sheet: "You can keep it if you want, it's for you."

But it was their turn now. Someone indicated to Claudio and Flavia that they could go in. Visitors to Griselda Solano, yes, that was it. The time had come to see her mother. Who for the moment lived there, far from them. Because she needed to rest.

RENÉ AND COLETTE

Ville-d'Avray

It was Flavia who gave me their contact details — "You should get in touch with them, they will explain the rest to you." She was talking about her primary school teacher, Colette and her partner René.

Flavia spoke to me at length about them on our first date: after that day, Colette and René had taken regular care of the little girl. The couple had no children. On weekends, on vacation, they took her with them. Like second parents. Or grandparents. Flavia didn't quite know how to put it.

After a long period during which both sides had lost touch, Flavia's parents had reconnected with René and Colette. Flavia wasn't sure how it came about, but the fact is that they had been seeing each other for some time. "Call them, it's important, they'll tell you things."

She was right, it was important.

I realized just how significant it was the very first time I went to visit René and Colette at their home in Ville-d'Avray.

They received me in the house where Colette has always lived, the very one where she was born. A gate, a slightly sloping garden, a millstone house hidden behind some trees, including a huge Lebanese cedar. It was on a lovely autumn day in November 2018, and beneath the big cedar tree the ground was covered in little brown and yellow cones.

"Colette calls them catkins, they're everywhere," René told me as he opened the garden gate.

On sunny days they like to sit under the big cedar. René immediately added that they had had lunch there with Claudio, Griselda and Flavia.

René knew that I had come to their house to learn about their relationship.

In Ville-d'Avray I encountered an endearingly messy house, a pavilion divided into several little rooms which you rarely see now as the trend is to remove partitions. We settled into a tiny living room cluttered with objects that looked like they had survived for well over half a century. It was one of those pre-Ikea interiors, where the dark wood furniture is still called loveseat or pedestal table and between which we had to weave our way. Seated around a table that was rather small and yet too big for the tiny room we were in (there was barely enough space for us to slip our bodies between the chairs and the tray), we drank coffee from flower cups then shared biscuits. Somewhere in the Ville-d'Avray house, as in Nerval's novellas, a clock ticked away the seconds.

It was during this visit to Ville-d'Avray that I found out about Colette's lost sight. The way it had happened, too: before we talked about Flavia and that day, about herself, Colette had felt the need to explain to me how it had come for her to no longer see anything at all.

The color of the sea

As old as she is, as a blind person Colette is a young blind person. Blindness came suddenly, a little over three years ago, without warning. Or barely any warning. Before the stroke that left her blind, there had just been a strange episode a few months earlier.

It was a beautiful day in June. Colette was sitting with her sister and René, on a Mediterranean beach somewhere near Saint-Raphaël. They were picnicking under the shelter of an umbrella, as the sun was beating down very hard; summer had indeed begun. The three of them were eating and chatting while looking at the sea and the boats. Suddenly, Colette had turned to her sister to ask her: "But why has the sea become so black, what do you call that phenomenon?" His sister had remained silent at first, not understanding the joke if it was one, then she had ended up muttering: "But what are you talking about, anyway... It's blue, the sea..." Colette had thought it was her sister who was playing a joke on her. This black sea before her eyes, this suddenly darkened atmosphere — not for a second had she imagined that she could be the only one to have seen it like that. Then she had insisted, with that Parisian accent that you hear now only in old films: "What do you call that phenomenon?" She remembered asking the question several times and repeating that word, *phenomenon*, convinced that it was the sea going dark, the moon playing tricks in the middle of the day, something to do with the stars or who knows what. There was surprise in her question, but also annoyance, as if she were asking the light and the colors to account for suddenly taking flight. Colette was surprised and protested at the same time, she wanted an explanation; her sister, who knew the region well, must know. "But this phenomenon... There, you see, it's all dark...," And then her sister repeated: "But what phenomenon are you talking about, what are you on about, Colette? You can see the sea clearly... It's there, in front of you, the sea is blue, the most beautiful turquoise, in fact..." The others didn't seem to understand what she was referring to. However, in the middle of the day and under the bright sun of an early summer, for Colette, the Mediterranean was black. As black as coal. But after a minute or two, everything was back to normal.

The light, the blue — all the colors, had suddenly returned to how they were. And Colette had not thought about it again.

Until the day where she stopped seeing anything at all.

It was after her stroke that Colette understood that what she had taken for a dialogue of the deaf on a beach on the Côte d'Azur was in fact a taste of her life as a blind person.

After her stroke, doctors told her she might regain her sight. A little, at least. But deep down, she didn't believe it.

"Now I'm in darkness all the time… Sometimes I can still see the light when it's really strong." I sometimes perceive things in brightness or rays…

After a silence, with a smile, nodding her head, she added: "I just have to get used to it, that's all."

As soon as I met her, Colette's voice struck me. It is surprisingly high-pitched and fresh for its age, slightly nasal, too. Beautiful, as she is.

René's notebooks

To orientate his memory and that of Colette, during my visit to Ville-d'Avray René went to look at the back of the house for two old shoeboxes where he keeps what he calls his *notebooks*. The first of them bears the date 1970 on the cover, the last to have been completed was filed in its shoebox only a few months ago.

René's *notebooks* are in fact small diaries that can be stored in the pocket of a painter's jacket. He always has one on him: in it he records appointments, trips, things he considers important as the days pass. Over a period of a week, there are sometimes two or three words, a first name, the name of a city. The space reserved for certain days, on the contrary, is full up: "lunch Maurice," "shopping," "post office," it makes him smile to reread himself today.

"Sometimes I have graphomaniac flare-ups, it seems... But when did it happen? The date of the events, I mean?

René also has a Parisian accent from another time, drawling and with a cheeky tone, à la Jean Gabin. He has the same way of holding his head when he speaks, white, close-cropped hair and blue eyes that reinforce the resemblance. His teeth are different, though: he has two very white and prominent incisors. René is an old Jean Gabin, but with two rabbit teeth.

"It happened in 1984. December 14, 1984."
"It was a Friday; I remember that very well. Wait until I show you..."

So, from one of his shoeboxes, René takes out the notebook corresponding to that year. He quickly turns the pages and arrives at the day in question. It was indeed a Friday. A simple name, in capital letters, occupies all the space reserved for Friday, December 14, 1984, written slightly diagonally and underscored with a double line. It is the surname of Claudio, Griselda and Flavia: SOLANO

Under the date for *that day*, there is nothing else in René's notebook. Nor is there anything for the following days. That Friday, he had written their name in his notebook. He had underlined it twice. Then, for days and days, he had written nothing more.

In their house in Ville-d'Avray, between the notebooks that René took out of the shoeboxes during the conversation, his memory and Colette's, a chronology appeared, that of their relationships with Flavia, Griselda and Claudio after that Friday in December 1984. In particular, that of their travels with Flavia, all those journeys that René and Colette made with the child after *the tragedy*.

On that day, Colette guessed that something had happened.

She remembers: Griselda stormed past her classroom in the middle of the day. She was haggard, her face covered in indecipherable make-up, wet from head to toe, as if she had fallen fully clothed into water. The woman standing before her seemed absent. So, even though this woman was the mother of the child she had come to pick up, Colette said: "No: class is not over, you cannot take your daughter."

Later, the sirens sounded. A fireman came, then a policeman. Bit by bit, she came to know what had happened.

Colette remembers: the day of the tragedy, when the bell had long since rung and all the other children had left, she stayed with Flavia. While she waited for someone to come to tell her to whom she should hand over the child, she tried to occupy her with some mathematical exercises.

Very soon after that day, René and Colette started taking Flavia for almost all the school holidays and often at weekends. Gradually they got to know Claudio. And later, Griselda.

"When she was with us, the little one always called me 'Mistress'. It was funny, she liked to call me that. She took a long time to call me by my first name. However, after the accident I no longer had her in my class. Flavia changed schools during the year. But even outside of school, and long after her preparatory class, she called me that. Even in adolescence. 'Mistress': for Flavia, that was my name."

Sometimes René and Colette talk about *the accident*. At other times it's *the tragedy*. Or *the drama*. René and Colette do not know what to call what happened that day.
 And neither do I.

During my visit to Ville-d'Avray, they listed the destinations and connected the images and anecdotes with the names and dates provided by René's notebooks. They seemed happy to reminisce about those journeys and initially followed their linear timeline. But around a memory or a detail that reminded them of another episode, they would reverse, go back in time or go far ahead in big leaps. René wandered through his notebooks, stopping suddenly at one page, pointing out a name or a detail with his index finger.

"There was Combloux and Sallanches, near the Aravis Mountains," Colette said.

Then René took out a new notebook and thumbed through it at full speed. Soon enough, he found the page he was looking for.

"There it is… Combloux, August 1988… Then there was Cherbourg, Barfleur and Saint-Vaast-la-Hougue."
 "It was good over there, it's awfully pretty, Saint-Vaast… And we had found a nice house," Colette said.
 "Yeah, we even went there several summers in a row. The last time… Wait until I show you…"

The Parisian accent of René and Colette is from another time. In truth, they speak a language that is almost extinct. It was in

Montmartre that René learned that Parisian accent. His way of speaking immediately surprised me. Each time he starts a new sentence, I am overwhelmed in advance.

Over the years I have lived in France, I have had the impression of having witnessed the slow disappearance of this way of speaking French, the extinction of its so particular cadence, as if it is swaying, with its so resonant rs, much thicker and less dry than those of today. The last time I heard this old Parisian language was already a long time ago. I was barely twenty years old. It was a shoemaker on the Rue du Temple, at the corner of Rue Saint-Merri, who spoke it still. I lived on this same street. I remember my fascination, I thought that this way of speaking no longer existed, that you could hear it only in old films. It is the language that is spoken in *French Cancan* by Jean Renoir, still in a few films shot in the 1960s, after which it is rarely heard on the screen. I remember being disconcerted and moved by it, to the point that when I had left the neighborhood, if I needed to have my shoes repaired, I would go as far as the Rue du Temple just to hear that way of speaking again. The shop is still there, but not the old cobbler. It had been so long since I had heard this language and its music — in real life, spoken live, I mean to say. That Colette and René speak like this, with the accent of the suburbs that no longer exist, gives them the air of very old sages.

René leafs through another notebook, then another. His index finger stops on a page, and he looks up at me, visibly pleased:

"...Found it! The last time at Saint-Vaast was in 1994. It seemed silly, these little notebooks, I looked like a right fool taking notes like that, eh, Colette? But you are interested by them. It wasn't so stupid, after all... It's all there..."

Before that, they had taken Flavia to Provins, Troyes and

Colombey-les-Deux-Églises. There had also been Saint-Dié and Gérardmer. Then they went to the Morvan, to Autun. Another time down by Dijon, in Beaune and Gevrey-Chambertin — "Like the wine, you see?" There had been so many places... Not to forget the weekends in Fontainebleau and the long walks around the ponds of Commelles and Mortefontaine, starting in the spring of 1985. In Nerval and Corot country.

"Shortly after the tragedy," René said.
    "Yes, just after the accident," Colette said.

Just a few weeks after that day.

Flavia especially liked to walk around the Château de la Reine Blanche. After their first visit, they often returned there. This place seemed to please the child so much.

"We went to pick up the kid, then we went for a walk in the forest of Chantilly."
    "She was wise and ever so cute. A little brunette, adorable. And she walked well, too. She never complained, you know? And if we were going to the forest and then to the Château de la Reine Blanche, in that case she would walk in front."
    "That's so true! She walked ahead of us..."

Flavia loved this place more than any other.
    On the site of the Château de la Reine Blanche, a building was erected in the Middle Ages. But most of what you see today was built in the 19th Century. With its turrets and pointed windows, in the heart of the forest, the Château de la Reine Blanche looks even more medieval than if it really were. It looks like the drawings that children make when they want to represent a

castle. "Have you been there yourself?" asked Colette.

I know the place, yes. Before Colette asked me the question, I even had the impression of seeing it very precisely in my mind. However, I have only been to the edge of these ponds once, near this castle lost in the forest and a very long time ago, I believe. But as soon as they named it, the places popped into my head. It's a site that you don't forget, probably because it looks like childhood.

René remembers: three knights decorate the facade and Flavia liked that René and Colette would imagine their adventures for her. The child liked this place so much that they usually picnicked there, in front of the pond, very close to the castle.

Flavia loved to eat by the water. And then, everything intrigued her.

First, that even if these bodies of water were called the Commelles ponds, they are actually in Coye-la-Forêt.

It was funny, every time Flavia said: "Coye-la-Forêt," Colette understood, from the child's intonation, that for her this place had the name of a question: "*Quoi, la forêt?*" or: "What, the forest?" No matter how much she explained to Flavia that "Coye" did not mean "what," that these two words weren't spelled the same at all, the child always said: "*Quoi, la forêt?.*" Then Colette and René laughed.

Colette felt that for Flavia this place looked like something out of a storybook. That being there, for her, was a bit like stepping into a fairy tale.

And then there was the name of that pond, very precisely. The pond at the edge of which sits the Château de la Reine Blanche. Because not only is this entire sector designated by the name of the Commelles ponds, when in fact we are in Coye-la-Forêt, in the Chantilly area. But in addition to that, the body of water in front of the castle bears the name of Étang de la Loge. It was really the weirdest thing in this story. "But, Mistress, where is the lodge?" Flavia always asked.

Then René and Colette explained to the child that the lodge in question, the one that had given its name to the pond, had nothing to do with the lodges that the child had known about, or with the one where she had lived. That they had read somewhere that when the Château de la Reine Blanche was built, a long time ago, but really a long, long time ago, there had been a lumberjack's or *bûcheron*'s lodge. "Hence the name," Rene explained.

The child then opened her eyes very wide. As if this lumberjack business was the ultimate confirmation. "A lumberjack's lodge, Mistress, is that why it's the Lodge's pond?" Is that it, Mistress? Because a long time ago there were lumberjacks in a lodge here at Quoi-la-Forêt?"

Through the forest, the three of them had indeed entered into a tale.

They told me all that, then Colette remained silent for a long time. The lodge, the water, the questions at Quoi-la-Forêt, that was a lot all at once. And the name of Commelles, how did Flavia hear it in her head? "*Comme elle?*" Before they first chose to picnic with Flavia near the Château de la Reine Blanche, they probably hadn't thought of it. But everything was there, condensed, at the edge of this pond. And Flavia who was seemingly magnetized by the place, this corner to which she always wanted to return. Where she asked Colette and René to speak to her, to tell her things. But what? They were incapable of retelling that day to the child. They would never have done it. The places spoke for them and something had led them there. In its own way, this corner of the forest told Flavia what adults were incapable of telling her, what they would never tell her. Not now, anyway. The silence continues. Colette is elsewhere.

She daydreams in the middle of darkness, in this great obscurity in which she moves. That darkness that is sometimes pierced by rays of light.

As she remains lost in thought, I try speaking to bring her back to us:

"It's good what you did… that after what happened you took her with you like that… Flavia told me a lot about the times spent with you. It meant a lot to her."

Then Colette turns to me, raising her unseeing eyes in my direction:

"Oh, you know… We didn't discuss it too much. We did things like that because we thought… that was the thing to do. That is all."

The Café in the Marais

I wanted to see René and Colette again.

They were also glad to see me: they had unearthed other memories and some photos that they wanted to show me. But for our second rendezvous, René and Colette wanted us to meet somewhere other than Ville-d'Avray, they wanted to spend a day in Paris.

So, I thought of Le Bûcheron.

Suddenly I saw signs everywhere.

Castle, lodge, pond, woodcutter. Marsh, forest, garden.

Basically, I knew all this meant nothing. Pure coincidence of names and places. If at the beginning of my investigation I had suggested to Flavia then to Griselda to meet at Le Bûcheron, it was only by chance.

But these words that kept returning in the notes that I had been taking for many months resonated like a tale within the story that I was pursuing.

There are often lumberjacks in the stories told to children. Sometimes they go deep into the forest to save a princess from danger. But other times, they are the ones who pose a threat.

So it was that inside the story that I was trying to reconstruct and understand, another seemed to be writing itself, all on its own.

And I also had to listen to that story. Because when things are given to be read in the form of a tale, we can go back to them again and again to try to unravel the mystery they contain.

I was thinking of Flavia, asking to return to the edge of the Lodge Pond, asking René and Colette to imagine just for her the destiny of the three knights of the Château de la Reine Blanche. I imagined Flavia listening to them while they picnicked together at the waterside, at Coye-la-Fôret. "*Quoi, la forêt?*" Near to the former woodcutters' lodge, which became this castle, the door of which was always closed.

Listening to Griselda, I had come to the edge of a chasm. Of the unbearable, the incomprehensible. Of dread.

But finding these words and objects as I carried out my investigation reassured me.

That is because stories do good things.

Stories are not only stories, essentially, they also alleviate.

Only there can the incomprehensible try to find a place for itself, there it can be brought together in its little melting pot. So that we can try to watch it now or later.

That's why on the telephone I suggested to René:

"Le Bûcheron, you know it?" It's in Saint-Paul, Rue de Rivoli, almost opposite the Metro.

"A café in the Marais? But that's all good!" replied René.

He seemed delighted; it had been a long time since they had been to the Marais, they particularly liked the area. "Colette may not come," René warned me, "she really wants a trip to Paris, but if on the day of our meet-up she does not feel well, I will come alone. She tires quickly, you know."

Despite the possible absence of Colette, I was happy that the place suited them. I was also hoping that we could sit at the table I had become accustomed to, the very one where I had listened to Flavia and then Griselda.

The time of chocolate

We set the date for January 31, 2019. It was a Thursday.

I entered Le Bûcheron by Rue du Roi-de-Sicile a few minutes before the agreed time.

The table I used for my previous interviews was free. I was able to sit in my usual place on the red banquette. The woman in the portrait was still there, impassive, in her gilded frame.

I had barely had time to take off my coat and open my notebook on the table when I saw René and Colette appear in front of the main entrance, the one which corresponds to the address I always give for my meetings at Le Bûcheron: 14, Rue de Rivoli. It's simple, the address is on the internet: "just click on the screen of a phone and Google will guide you to the café." Le Bûcheron is almost opposite the Metro: "if you get off at Saint-Paul, all you have to do is cross the street and take a few steps towards the Tour Saint-Jacques," that's what I always say. Nothing could be easier. Even tourists know the Rue de Rivoli. But I prefer to use the other entrance, the tiny door that opens onto Rue du Roi-de-Sicile. First of all because I normally arrive by foot, from the Haut Marais where I live, but also because I like the idea of the hidden entrance. The regulars come in by the hidden entry, the secret doorway the existence of which you only know if you have already visited Le Bûcheron. The one, above all, which does not correspond to the address of the café and which gives me the impression, despite the agitation and the ambient noise, of meeting guests in my own territory. This other entrance opens onto a slightly raised space, where there are a few tables to the side, between the door overlooking the Rue du Roi-de-Sicile and a tiny open kitchen. A few steps lead down to the room in the form of a long corridor where *my* table is.

Seeing René and Colette arrive together, I felt myself smiling as I gave René a big wave of my arm, both to get him to spot me and to let him know that I was really happy to see the two of them.

Colette let René guide her through the narrow passage that separates the counter from the single row of tables. Holding one another by the arm, they advanced slowly towards me, following the slight swinging movement of her chest.

On January 31, 2019, Colette wore padded white sneakers like a teenager would wear, a colorful dress, a waistcoat on top and a woolen coat that looked a bit like a cape. Her fair hair was pressed into several large curls held by a sort of headband above her perfectly bare forehead. If it weren't for her huge sneakers, she would have looked like a fairy godmother. The good fairy of the vanished suburbs. Colette is small in stature, slightly stooped, she has large, almost translucent light blue eyes, and extremely white skin that catches light as easily as it reflects it.

Barely arrived in front of me, René moved the table then pushed aside two chairs, trying as best he could with his hands and elbows to guide Colette to the bench.

I suddenly got up, made a few hasty gestures to help them and immediately regretted having chosen such an inconvenient place for a blind old lady. All because I had let myself get caught up in the delirium of signs.

I immediately thought it's the crazy ones who see signs everywhere. Those who believe that around them tales write themselves, stories that they only have to pick up to understand everything, to uncover what is hidden from them.

I should have chosen another place for René and Colette.

I was ashamed of not having taken the initiative, of not getting up earlier, of having stood still watching them, captivated as I was by their appearance and the light that emanated from Colette.

So many tables and chairs in a long, narrow room, not forgetting the steep staircase that leads to the basement toilets, a staircase that those who cannot see would not be aware of. And when Colette was finally taking her place, I realized that even as I gave René a friendly wave, she was passing inches from the open hopper in the floor. Luckily René was acting as a scout and she was following in his footsteps, otherwise she could have disappeared into the hole and rolled all the way down. This tale that was writing itself had its scapegoat. Le Bûcheron, what an idea that was… Because of me, Colette could have hurt herself.

She moved with difficulty. She still hadn't finished taking off her coat when I saw a waitress pulling in her stomach and swaying her hips behind René, contorting her upper body to place two steaming cups on a table next to ours — the cups passed over Colette's curly hair, under the nose of the woman in the portrait, and I feared an imminent disaster. It seemed like René could read my thoughts as he straight away gave me a reassuring smile. He was in control of the situation, there was no need to worry.

René's gestures were both quick and precise, always very gentle and kind. Despite the noise that rung out at Le Bûcheron, in this Parisian space that suddenly seemed so cramped and aggressive to me, when Colette finished settling in she was as

smiling and radiant as the first time I had seen her.
"For me, it will be a hot chocolate!"

She pronounced these words in a childish tone, as if amused.
"A hot chocolate? Now there's a good idea," said René.

The three of us laughed for a long time, without really knowing why. Everything seemed so complicated and simple at the same time. As the waitress approached I opened my notebook, as had become my habit.

Colette couldn't stop smiling, her blue eyes laughing on their own. When her hot chocolate finally arrived, I had a ninety-year-old little girl in front of me.

FLAVIA

Infelix amor. *What love saved*

Flavia fascinates me.
 The woman she has become. The peaceful assurance with which she speaks.
 I would like to say that she is strong, but I do not have words great enough to express this force, no words to match up to her.
 Flavia.
 She has a strength and a courage in her that I never thought could exist.
 I've known it all along: I am writing this book for her.
 I write for the little girl she was and still is.
 I'm writing for the child who has kept within her, for more than thirty years, four images of that day. Who then delivered them to me at a café table.
 From our first meeting at Le Bûcheron, Flavia spoke of the mother that Griselda was to her for all those years.

"Present, loving. Very loving."

She looked me in the eye as she said those words. To make sure I heard, to let me know she didn't say those words lightly.
"Loving, truly."
 I try to understand. I believe her.

It will soon be three years since that first meeting. It will soon be three years that I have been looking for the way to write this book. To get closer to what happened to them without hurting them, without adding pain to pain. But also certain that I must complete what I have undertaken, that I must go to the end of this attempt to understand their story.

It will soon be three years that I have been trying to get there. I took a lot of notes, notebook upon notebook. I questioned, read, listened. I looked for stories that have commonalities with that of Griselda. Very old stories, sometimes. I read and reread Medea, Seneca's play and Euripides' play. What Ovid says about Medea in *The Metamorphoses*. I often thought of Flavia listening to this same story, sitting in silence next to Sylvain. This story of passion, madness, violence and death — exile, too. For a long time, this book was called *Infelix amor*, unhappy love. A few words that Medea utters in Seneca's play: *Saevit infelix amor*, these are the words that Medea puts to her madness and pain, and in the conciseness of the Latin so many questions remain open. *It burns me, my unhappy love*, in Arnaud Fabre's translation. *It was my love that was unleashed to become devastating*, in Blandine Le Callet's version. *Unhappy love rages*, that's what it could look like in the simple Latin dear to Pascal Quignard.

But Griselda is not Medea. And the main reason for their difference is the existence of Flavia.

I know why this book I am writing means so much to me: for that which love has saved. For the child who escaped that day and whom love carried and made grow. For what Flavia is today.

I have read essays and studies on infanticidal mothers.

Watched and rewatched Martin Scorsese's *Shutter Island*, the film inspired by Dennis Lehane's novel. The scene at the lake in front of which Andrew Laeddis finds his wife. She is in a swing, barefoot, like she's dazed. Her hair is wet, her dress too. Before her is the lake where Dolores Chanal/Rachel Solando has just drowned her three children. A girl, the eldest, and two boys whom the father, mad with pain, pulls out of the water before laying them on the grass.

I read various articles that appeared in the press. Here, elsewhere. The horror of a story repeating itself.

Unlike Medea, most of these mothers kill by suffocating, drowning or freezing. Without bloodshed. As if they were trying to shelter their child's body, to slip it into a protective cocoon — water, ice. It often happens that after killing the mother wraps the body of her child in cloths. That she puts it into a bathrobe. In a desire for preservation gone mad and murderous.

Griselda spent only a few months in prison. Nine months, to be precise.

This short period of imprisonment is the result of chance, not of sentencing. It is the time it took the lawyer in charge of the case to get Griselda out of the remand center where she was detained in order to get her into a psychiatric hospital. This is what she strove to obtain as soon as she was entrusted with the file — but it was exactly nine months after the fact that the lawyer succeeded in having Griselda committed to the Maison Blanche. Nine months, the time of a pregnancy: the chronology set by chance is disturbing. Was she born to herself, otherwise, after this time of imprisonment? Was Griselda born otherwise to her daughter?

Thanks to Flavia, I learned the name of the lawyer who had defended Griselda and got in touch with her. "I remember this case like it was yesterday," was the first thing she said to me over the phone. She repeated this same sentence when we met up. But before continuing, she asked me: "And Flavia, how is she?" I gave her the latest news I had. The lawyer wanted me to talk about her work, her photographs. "She's a wonderful girl, isn't she?" It wasn't a real question; the lawyer just wanted us to talk about what Flavia had become before talking about that day and her role in this case. "Yes, she's wonderful, much more than that, in truth," I replied. The lawyer was happy. Proud, even, to have made this possible. Then she started telling me about what had happened.

She was immediately persuaded that Griselda's place was in a psychiatric hospital and not in a cell. But this hospitalization that she had ended up obtaining had been like a tour de force. She still remembers the energy she had deployed to make this happen. "I didn't give up, I moved heaven and earth, really, I felt like I was moving more than mountains, volcanoes." It was one of her first cases; she was a very young lawyer at the time.

At the trial, which took place a year and a half after the events, Griselda arrived free. And she came out free too since she was given a five year suspended prison sentence. "If we were to say that this penalty punishes a double infanticide by drowning in a bathtub, there is certainly reason to be stunned," said one of the articles published in the press after the trial. But the gamble behind this extremely lenient verdict was to give Flavia a chance. She was there, alive, she had survived that day. And she needed her mother. This is of what the very young lawyer had succeeded in convincing the judge and the jury: that they had to give Griselda the chance to be a mother for Flavia. *She will be, you will see.* The time that followed seemed to prove her right.

"She was a present, loving mother. Very loving."

I suddenly think of Flavia saying these words.

I can only record what I have seen and heard.

In the darkest place, in the depths of night and horror, they placed a bet on love and life.

The birthday cake

During our first meeting at Le Bûcheron, I had told Flavia that I was surprised that her parents had not separated after that day. Because Claudio still lives with Griselda, in the apartment he found while she was still in prison, before being admitted to a psychiatric hospital. It was from this same apartment that Flavia and Claudio used to leave to go and see Griselda: *where Mama is resting*. And later in the hospital. Griselda and Claudio never moved.

It was in this same apartment that I attended Claudio's birthday with Flavia, Griselda and a friend of theirs, by which point I had been working on this book for a long time. Claudio was celebrating his eighty-eighth birthday, it was afternoon. I had arranged with Flavia to meet up before going to her parents' house together. Flavia bought a cake from a bakery that is almost opposite their building, a very colorful fruit tart: "all those colors should make my father happy." I picked up a bottle at a nearby wine shop.

Griselda seemed happy to see Flavia and I arriving together. She showed us her latest paintings and some sculptures. It was at the hospital, Maison-Blanche, that she had resumed painting. Claudio had turned up one day with colors and brushes, canvases, an easel. She had resumed painting, as before, in La Plata. And she hasn't stopped since. Griselda has set up her studio in Flavia's old bedroom — this is where she spends most of her days.

Claudio sat down at one end of the table, Flavia cut the cake, opened the bottle then she served everyone. She was smiling, playful, visibly happy with this improvised snack in honor of her father.

The table was small, the room too, we were all seated in front of small plates, very close to each other. We talked about everything and nothing. Then Flavia took her cellphone and photographed Claudio in front of his slice of cake and full glass. I didn't notice straight away, but Claudio's face had been turned towards his daughter for quite a long time.

I have often looked at the photo taken by Flavia on the occasion of her father's eighty-eighth birthday.

Claudio appears on the left of the image, in a small-checked shirt open over a gray T-shirt, seated at the table set for his birthday. He has white, wavy hair that reaches his shoulders and is reminiscent of those beautiful, long curls often seen in male portraits of the Italian Renaissance. I'm particularly thinking of a self-portrait by Raphael — although it's white, it's like Claudio's hair is that of a young man enjoying his own renaissance. While Griselda does not appear in this shot, it took this photo for me to become aware of the contrast between their two hairstyles, the close-cropped hair of one and the abundant hair of the other. A light beard and mustache barely cover Claudio's skin. On his face they form a thin, almost translucent veil. He wears rectangular metal-rimmed glasses that add to the effects of transparency in the image, with the stemmed glass, just filled, in the foreground. He didn't touch it. In an instant, just with her phone, Flavia composed a striking portrait. What is most remarkable in this image is Claudio's attitude: in front of his slice of cake and the glass of alcohol that his daughter has just served him, his face turns to her, his hands are on his knees, like a well-behaved boy. He is waiting. It's almost like he has no intention of moving. Claudio's body and face seem frozen. But he is not posing. This immobility says something else. Looking at this photo, one can understand that Flavia captured in her father one of those moments when the body reveals truths as deep as they are difficult to formulate. Or else things that end up being said because the body has taken over.

Claudio seems separate from everything around him. The cake on the plate with its golden border. The spoon. The glass and the translucent liquid that also give off golden glints. The trinkets behind him, the puppet hanging from a doorknob. The moment Flavia takes this photo it seems that for Claudio none of this exists. Even his own body, installed there on the chair, in front of the tea prepared for his eighty-eighth birthday. It looks like a still life; everything seems fixed for evermore. It looks like no one will eat this cake, no one will drink this glass of wine. Especially not Claudio. He carries an extremely heavy bundle on his shoulders, a load that has petrified him forever. The only living things in this photo are Flavia's father's eyes. They are all the more striking. Claudio's eyes, turned towards the phone. They come from another time. They are placed on his daughter; it is to her that they are addressed. Claudio cannot say anything, he just can't, but something is said in his gaze. And what those eyes say to Flavia is that you should not blame her. His eyes apologize, but the pain is too great. As great as the love with which he looks at his daughter — who also has her eyes on her father, on the other side of the phone.

At T. High School

Together, Flavia and I are trying to move closer to that day.

For her, it is a necessity. She told me that on our first meeting. For a long time, that day was in her memory as only a shard of mute rock; but for some months, she has finally dared to look at it. To name it. After pretending none of this had happened, in a mixture of dread and shame (yes, shame, it's weird but she, Flavia, has long been paralyzed by endless shame), she finally told her close friends about it. But between her mother and her, it is always impossible to broach the subject. Unthinkable.

My book will help her, she thought. Will help them. Maybe.

With my questions and our meetings at Le Bûcheron, I came at just the right time. And then her mother wanted to talk — to me.

"I don't know what you said to each other when you met up with each other... She stayed with you for a long time here at the café, didn't she?"

"Yes. Until the moment when we really had to leave, we were almost kicked out..."

"That same evening I called her. And she seemed relaxed, happy... It did her good to talk to you."

Flavia smiled.

"Hurry up and get it all together... When do you think you'll be done? When do you think your book will come out?"

Suddenly, Flavia seemed very impatient to see me finish this book, that I get to the end of this story.

"I don't know, I can't know. I have to write it yet. My publisher has to want my book, too. I don't control much, as it happens..."

I paid for our two coffees then we headed for the exit onto Rue de Rivoli.

"Anyway, regarding the high school, I'm working on it."

Flavia wanted us to go to T. High School together.

It had been so long since she had been back there. She wondered if they would let us in. "Schools have become kinds of fortresses," she said. She thought that it would probably be necessary to start by making a request to the management, that it would likely be complicated. But she wanted to see the place again and she felt that it was important for the book I wished to write. She intended to take the opportunity to take some pictures, especially of the small garden that had meant so much to them all, even if she feared that there was not very much of it left.

These places where Flavia lived until she was six, the places that saw: *that day*. It was in a viewfinder that she first imagined finding them, separated from them by a camera and a lens.

"Do you think this will work? And that they'll be okay with me taking pictures?"

By mutual agreement we decided that I would take care of the arrangements so that we could go to T. High School together.

"I'll contact them, I'll let you know their response."

As soon as I got home, I wrote a long email to the principal of T. High School, saying that I was a writer and that I was interested in the story of Flavia Solano, someone who had lived in the institution she was in charge of today, but in the 1980s. That her parents, at the time, worked in the school as caretakers. That Flavia not only knew about the request I was making, but that she would come with me. That, moreover, she wanted to take some pictures, if the headmistress gave her permission. I clarified: "Flavia Solano is a professional photographer." I even included a link to Flavia's work in my email.

The principal of T. High School answered me immediately. Not only did she know perfectly well who Flavia was, but when she started in the establishment, the Solanos were still living there. The principal was very young at the time, the Solanos still occupied the small lodge on the ground floor when she took her first steps as a teacher at T. High School, an establishment she has never since left.

The principal therefore knew their story. She knew about that day. The details she gave me about her early days at T. High School were a way of making me understand.

But in her message she was content just to say that she knew perfectly well who Flavia Solano was, that she had known her from a very young age, and: "of course, I would be delighted to welcome you both."

Nothing else.

No reference in her email to any event. No "pain," no "tragedy," no "misfortune" mentioned in her message about the departure of the Solanos. Nothing but the confirmation that she knew about the event that she did not name any more than she mentioned it.

I imagined her writing her email to answer me.

Perhaps she had written a sentence with one of these words: "I know perfectly well who Flavia Solano is, I had just joined the establishment when the terrible misfortune which forced them to leave touched her family."

Then I imagined her erasing it immediately. No, not *misfortune*, not that word…

Perhaps she immediately went for: "I know perfectly well who Flavia Solano is, I had just joined the establishment when the *tragedy*…" No, not the *tragedy*. The *accident*?

No, not the accident, it was not an accident.

So, the principal preferred this simple statement, telling herself that I would understand it that way, that I would mentally complete things: "When I joined the establishment, they lived there, in the lodge."

The speed with which her response came, the words she chose were full of delicacy.

She had probably understood what prompted me to get in touch with her.

But in truth, I had not said much either.

The principal most likely understood that I was writing about that day. That Flavia knew. That she even agreed, since the little girl she had known, who had become a forty-year-old woman, would come with me. Perhaps she had guessed that at Le Bûcheron, a few hours before I wrote my email, Flavia had said to me:

"You know, I don't mind you writing about our story. Neither does my mother, I don't think it bothers her. In fact…"

We were seated under the portrait of the woman with the bun.

Flavia was installed exactly where her mother had been a few days earlier, exactly where Griselda had told me her story, in one go. And suddenly everything made sense. The words Flavia was saying, my notebook open on the coffee table, all around us. Times and voices merged.

"I think I need you to write this book. And my mother too. That she will tell me through you what happened. You have to write so that I finally know."

Yes, the principal might have imagined something like that conversation we had, Flavia and I. Her answer which said almost nothing said it all: "When I joined the establishment, they were living there, in the lodge… I would be delighted to welcome both of you. Of course, she can take all the photos she wants."

I arrived a little before our appointed time. It was a Wednesday.

A text from Flavia told me: "I'll be a little late."

I took the opportunity to survey the street, locate the places. The high school where the Solanos lived is in fact almost opposite the school where Flavia started her preparatory class, on both sides of the same short and narrow street. Everything there feels tight, narrow.

I had also known this place, but I have a vague, distant memory of it. I have not set foot on this street since 1982, even though I have lived in the Paris region and then inner Paris without interruption for many years. While waiting for Flavia, I try to reactivate images, to see if this gate or this piece of sidewalk awakens a buried memory in me. But the memories remain as distant and vague, after all these years, before this closed door.

When it's time for the meeting, Flavia is still not there, and I hesitate before ringing the bell. I don't want to go into the school without her. At the same time, I am afraid that her delay will affect our visit. So, I decide to go in, say a word to the guard: "I have an appointment, but I'm expecting another person who isn't here yet." She allows me to stay in the vestibule.

I imagine that this visit is very hard for Flavia, I fear a very long delay. I imagine her getting ready in the morning, hesitating. The minutes keep ticking by, I begin to think that Flavia may not come.

But she eventually arrives. When she enters the vestibule where I'm seated, she looks smiling, relaxed. I am reassured. But she has a very small bag with her, because Flavia didn't take her photographic equipment, whereas at Le Bûcheron she had spoken to me at length about the photos she wanted to take and her fear that she wouldn't be allowed to.

The principal receives us in her office.

She remembers Flavia when she was just six years old. Then come the usual phrases about the passage of time, so annoying to hear when you are very young or still in adolescence

("But it's hard to believe," "I see you still very small, with a clip in your hair," "You were this tall"). These inevitable clichés that one day we surprise ourselves by repeating, surprised that they are not only commonplaces, but that these sentences can also say moving and meaningful things.

The principal asks after Flavia's father, talks to her about the imprint he left on the establishment, where they strive to respect the bright colors he had chosen *in his time* for the walls and doors.

"Every time we paint the doors orange or purple, we say to each other that those are the colors Mr. Claudio had chosen." It is as if he were still there, as if regularly, every three or four years, he himself repainted for the umpteenth time the walls of the school and the doors of the classrooms.

The principal asks about Claudio, who worked in the establishment for a long time. You see, after that day Claudio continued to do maintenance work in the school, until his retirement. For years after the events, he surveyed this same courtyard, picked up the leaves from beneath these same trees.

The names of Boris and Sacha are not mentioned, or that of Griselda either. Almost like in the lodge, Flavia and Claudio lived alone. That day of which no one speaks, seems to make the evocation of Griselda and her sons perfectly impossible. As if at the end of that day, in the depths of its darkness and its unbearable mystery, Boris, Sacha and Griselda had disappeared. Together.

I listen in silence to the conversation between the principal and Flavia, throwing in a question from time to time — a name, a date that I ask them to confirm. I take notes, like a scrupulous and discreet clerk.

We walk through the hallways. Some classes are occupied by students. They practice the visual arts there; the school has several art sections. On the ground floor, there is a ceramic plaque: *Art*

Flower Workshop. We enter the room because it is unoccupied. The tables are mounted on trestles, everywhere we see the remains of fabric and crepe paper, small transparent pots with ribbons, buttons and pearls.

Then we approach the former lodge.

Flavia is calm, relaxed, with a calmness that surprises me.

"Your old apartment is occupied by offices now. The place probably no longer looks like you knew it…"

The principal asks Flavia if she wants to enter the old lodge. But Flavia refuses. A barely audible: "No," which she confirms with a slight shake of her head. No, she doesn't want to. At all.

I understand at that moment why she did not take her camera.

The few steps leading to the lodge, I think I recognize them. How many times did I go to T. High School when my dad was living with the Solanos? How many times have I myself climbed those steps that Flavia, next to me, no longer wants to tread, those steps that keep her at a distance like an impassable barrier? I am unaware of it, but these places speak to me. The columned promenade in front of the glass doors of the current offices, too. But I say nothing. There are times like this when you can only watch, listen to the noises of the city, near and far at the same time and then be silent.

RENÉ, COLETTE AND FLAVIA

Pictures of Flavia.
Kaddish for Gilbert Bloch

I see René for the third time. He found old photos of Flavia. He had the idea to scan them and print them to give me a copy. "It might help you. You'll see, some are beautiful," he told me on the phone, before our meeting. In the album he has prepared, the photos are arranged in chronological order.

Fontainebleau, 1985: Flavia is seated on a rock, she wears a pink T-shirt and brandishes a piece of wood in her right hand, vertically, like a conductor between two movements.

Trouville, 1986: Flavia wears an anorak, rubber boots, a white balaclava. The sea is less than a meter away from her. The strip of sand on which the child is standing is rust colored, of a surprising hue. "They are old photos, the colors have faded," says René. On the orange sand, at Flavia's feet, the pebbles and shells gleam golden in the light.

Same place, same year, but another day this time because Trouville beach is covered in snow: Flavia is from behind and Colette a few meters from her, crouching. They seem to be throwing snowballs at each other. Flavia's shadow stretches out in front of her, as if she were a giant. Crouching as she is, Colette seems very small compared to the child: the shadow of Flavia's legs rises up to Colette for at least two meters, like two long rails on the snow. But the child's body does not stop there, its shadow covers part of

Colette's coat and continues behind her, for more than a meter.

Morvan, 1987: Flavia is sitting on a swing, as is René, side by side, like two children ready to take off. Flavia wears glasses that seem held together by a rubber band.

Cotentin, 1990, another swing on which Flavia is standing this time. Her glasses are black, her hair much longer. In her white dress, with ankle socks of the same color, she looks defiantly at the camera; next to her, René is mounted on a rope and wooden ladder, he puts his head between two bars, looking amused, but he seems less stable than the child, he seems to be struggling to keep his balance.

Only the first photo in the series does not follow the chronological order. René is proud to show it to me and to point out: this photo is special, it's like the cover of his Flavia picture book.
 "I didn't miss that one, did I? Right, I didn't miss it?"

Cherbourg, 1992: Flavia is perched on something that looks like a block of granite. Behind her you see an all-white ocean liner. She wears a white, ruffled, sleeveless dress. It is summer. Flavia stands straight with her hands behind her back and her left leg at the side, in what dancers call the second position. But it is the crane behind her that makes the photo so surprising. The machine's arm is folded in the direction of the child's head and, by an optical illusion, it looks like the chain hanging from the carriage is holding the child by the top of her skull.
 "Look at that crane in the port of Cherbourg. It looks like it is there, just for her! She couldn't fall, the kid huh, she couldn't!"

The most surprising thing, René explains to me, is the way he and Colette got back in touch with Claudio and Griselda a few years ago. René asks me if I know… When I say that I don't know, he tells me.

"We hadn't seen them for a long time. When Flavia became a teenager, I don't know… Colette and I felt that she needed us less. Or maybe she needed something else. Colette had been so close to what happened… And since after that we had taken the little one almost every weekend and during all the school holidays, we were there all the time, you see… We spent wonderful moments with her but, suddenly, we felt… That all three of them wanted us to step back, that they no longer wanted us in their hair all the time. Colette thought that she reminded them of things they wanted to forget… I don't really know, to be honest. In any case, at one point we stopped taking Flavia and at the same time we no longer saw the parents… Then one day… It was in 2008, in December, I recall. A friend of mine had died. Gilbert Bloch, a mountaineer friend that I liked very much. The funeral took place in Pantin, in one of the Jewish divisions of the cemetery. And there… to be honest, I don't really know what happened. I believe that it is the Kaddish that explains everything. The true Kaddish of the bereaved. I had never heard it. Have you ever heard the Kaddish? For me, it was the first time. And to tell you the emotion that I felt… It just came up, suddenly. I can't explain it. I still have goosebumps, just telling you about it, look… goosebumps… So, after the ceremony for Bloch, I didn't leave with the others. I excused myself, then I went to the reception. I knew the Solano children were there too. I had never seen their grave but I knew they were in Pantin. Suddenly… it was like all the moments we had spent with Flavia, they were for them too. I wanted to tell them, you know? So, I asked the guard where the Solano children were… It's strange, but it was really the Kaddish, it was the Kaddish that pushed me…"

The children are together. Everything could not be simpler, René says. And there are two rosebushes there. Just by seeing them, he knew that it was Claudio who had chosen and planted them.

In front of the children's grave, he meditated.

René knows nothing about Jewish prayers, but what he said that day in his head, the words he addressed to the children were still full of echoes of the Kaddish. And there was nothing sad in that, no, there was no question of death, there was no question of the end, on the contrary… The words he said to the children that day were beautiful, they were filled with light.

When he finished meditating, without really knowing why, René tore a page from the notebook that, as usual, he had with him. He wrote on it his first name, his email address, his mobile number. And he stuck it on one of the thorns of the smallest rosebush.

"Three days later, I got a phone call. It was Griselda… It must have been fifteen years… Obviously, she had found my little piece of paper planted on the rosebush. But for her to have found it in the middle of December… She must go there often, to the little ones' grave… A piece of paper stuck on a rosebush thorn at the beginning of winter, think about that a little… This is the kind of thing that the rain and the wind carry away. Really, it had no chance, my little piece of paper. Yet she found it… But she didn't say anything, you see. She just called, like that, without saying why she was doing it, without saying how she got my number, after all this time… Then we saw each other… Without explaining or justifying anything, as if we had never stopped seeing each other. And we meet up now from time to time. They sometimes come to our home. When the weather is nice, we eat at the place that you know, under the trees. Where there are the catkins that Colette loves so much, under the big cedar tree, remember?"

I know Flavia is crying into her phone.

She did not know how her parents had reconnected with René and Colette after so many years. I have just told her. And I know she is crying, that she can't stop crying.

She didn't know about the Kaddish any more than the roses. Flavia had never seen her brothers' graves. And her mother goes there. Often...

Flavia is crying.

Because she just realized something. She lives in Pantin. Barely a hundred meters from the cemetery.

It was only recently that she chose to settle there.

This is the first apartment that is really hers: she managed to buy it. This is the place she chose to live, the first place she wanted for herself.

She must have known, yes, that her brothers were also in Pantin. She vaguely knew, yes. She had heard it before, a long time ago, maybe it's coming back to her, now that she thinks about it... But this grave that she has never seen... Boris and Sacha, there, a few meters from her home ... Only now does she understand.

Pantin. Afternoon tea. On all fours

Colette and René pick me up by car, downstairs from my home.

We have an appointment in Pantin with Flavia, in her street, at the foot of her building.

Flavia gets into René and Colette's car. We are, however, very close to the cemetery. But this is how things are, as if we have a long road ahead. Flavia kisses René and Colette, she kisses me too and adjusts her belt next to me. He starts the car, off we go.

Then René parks his car and the four of us get out, barely a hundred meters from Flavia's home.

It is November, a beautiful autumn day, cool but clear, the surrounding air is full of golden light.

René prepared the visit. He knows exactly the location of the grave we are looking for. It is a single plot, Boris and Sacha were buried there together.

Spontaneously, Flavia, René and I begin to describe the place aloud, so that Colette can see with us.

"It's a very simple grave, in the ground."

"There's just a white wooden cross. Undated."

"A very old cross. My father must have found it at a flea market."

"No date is given, it's an ageless grave… It is thirty-four years old, but it could be fifty, a hundred or more. There are just two first names drawn in black ink, *Boris* and, below, *Sacha*. No surname".

"I think it's Papa's handwriting."

Colette listens in silence. She feels the water under her feet.

"It has been raining a lot, it seems… I can see… There, it's shining…"

Colette is proud to show us that she manages to see the water in the puddles at her feet, that she can also participate in the description of the scene. She insists and I am surprised: I thought she saw the lights only when they were really bright. It seems that the water in the puddles shines with a light that only Colette is able to perceive.

Then we head to the exit and walk to the car. We are going only as far as Flavia's place, her apartment a hundred meters away. But that is how things are.

I help Colette to settle in the front, I get in the back with Flavia. We fasten our seat belts. That's it, we are ready to go.

With the doors barely closed and after a short silence we start talking as if we had just met up.

"I live on the fifth floor, no elevator. Are you two okay?"
"Of course, we will be fine!"
It is René who speaks.

Colette climbs while holding onto René's arm, slowly but without stopping. I see her face turned towards Flavia and me who are already one floor higher on the fifth. Colette smiles under her curly hair.

"Well, you see, we're just coming…"

Flavia's apartment is very colorful. I say to her that the colors in the light from the fifth floor are very vivid.

"But the most beautiful color is on one of the walls of my room, you can't see it from here, I'll show you… I thought I wasn't going to dare, but… look, it's beautiful, no?"

"Yes, very. You were right to dare to have this color."

Flavia made crêpes. She pulls out several jars of jam. She asks us what we would like to drink with it.

As usual, Colette asks if she can have a hot chocolate.

Colette is radiant. And very playful, suddenly. Quite proud to have climbed the five floors up to the apartment of her former preparatory class student. Then to have afternoon tea there, quietly installed at Flavia's, a cup of hot chocolate in hand.

"I amazed you on that one, admit it…"

"It's true, you amazed me, at the top of the stairs you were barely out of breath."

"You know, when I lost my sight, I had to learn to fend for myself. The stairs, I tame them, the stairs, they don't scare me! At home, when René is not there, I go up them on all fours…"

Colette waves her arms like a kid. Watching her mime sequence, Flavia's face lights up. Suddenly, I see the little girl playing on the beach at Trouville with her Mistress. Colette does it some more, Flavia squints. Now she is laughing out loud.

"But not to get down, surely? To get down, that can't work!"

"Of course it can, Flavia! Perfectly! Backwards, and even upside down. I'm in control of my situation, you'd better believe it"

Then Colette waves her arms even more. As if she were launching herself down an imaginary staircase.

This time, the three of us laugh for a long time. Everything seems so complicated and simple at the same time.

Then Colette stops. She's radiant, like a mischievous little girl, happy with the scene she has just played out for us.

*

Griselda goes to the Pantin cemetery. Often.

How many times per year? Per month? Per week?

We cannot measure, impossible to count.

She has been making this journey for years. Since that day, she hasn't stopped making it.

Griselda gets off at Aubervilliers — Pantin — Quatre-Chemins Metro station. It is on line seven. The pink line which, with its fork at one end, looks a bit like an arrow. But Griselda travels in the opposite direction, away from the fork, to where the line stretches straight ahead.

She knows the route by heart. Once you go past the gate, you enter the forest.

Griselda knows every tree that leads to Boris and Sacha. They give their names to the passageways: Avenue des Marronniers-Rouges, Avenue des Noisetiers-de-Byzance, Avenue des Érables-Pourpres, Avenue des Tilleuls-de-Hollande. But these are not avenues. Just paths that crisscross the forest, equidistant from heaven and earth.

Having arrived in front of Boris and Sacha's grave, Griselda takes care of the rosebushes. She waters them, prunes them if they need pruning. She removes the dead leaves when it's the season, takes away the faded flowers if that is what has to be done. When the rosebushes are in bud, she watches them very closely, the caterpillars should not interrupt the flowering. Griselda takes care of the roses. She takes care of what she needs to take care of, in silence. That is why she goes alone to Pantin. It is very important that she be alone.

Flavia lives nearby now. She is close. Does she know? Griselda wonders. Yes, of course she does.

Since Flavia lives in Pantin, so close to the boys, Griselda often thinks of the children's mezzanine. The one that Claudio himself had set up in their lodge at the same time as theirs, the adults' mezzanine, so that the five of them could live in there.

She sees the children again, up there.

On their mezzanine, Claudio and Griselda were so close to their children. It was simple, she just had to get up very slightly on her bed to see them.

These mezzanines looked like two huge rafts. In their lodge, there was the adults' raft and the children's one.

If another person had to describe the image that Griselda sees right now — the very specific image she has in her head when she thinks about all this — would that other person have said that the two rafts of the lodge at T. High School were side by side? Or else one behind the other? She doesn't know what words another person would have chosen.

But Griselda has no doubts about it.

The children are in front. Necessarily.

The children always run ahead.

This book is inspired by real events. The identities have been changed intentionally as well as certain circumstances in order to protect the current lives of the people in question.

WITH THANKS

To the real people who inspired the characters of Flavia, Griselda, René, Colette, Janine and the lawyer, for the time they dedicated to me, for the confidence and the courage with which they shared so many memories with me.

To my editor Jean-Marie Laclavetine, for his advice, his patience and his constant support. To Anne Vijoux, for listening and looking.

To Olga Grumberg and Cathy Vidalou, for listening to me and reading me — always loyal, for so many years.

To Hélène, my first reader.

To Jean-Baptiste, Augustin and Émilien.